# ONE
# GOOD
# STORY

By Ron Severs

ISBN 0-931714-89-3

First Edition

Library of Congress Number: 00-108791

NODIN PRESS
a division of Micawber's Inc.
525 North Third Street
Minneapolis, MN 55401

Printed by Printing Enterprises

# ONE
# GOOD
# STORY

# Acknowledgements

ONE GOOD STORY is the result of encouragement and support from so many wonderful people. The author wishes to thank all who have played a role in making this book possible.

River people are the most trusting and giving people I have ever met. Their kindness, support, and wide-eyed enthusiasm for 'another story' about an encounter on the river; a hearty slap on the back while saying, 'Man, I wish I were doing that;' or that genuine handshake followed by a sincere 'good luck' or 'be careful,' were many times the impetus to keeping me going. If I have mixed up some names I apologize—there were so many great people. To all the river people, I say "Thank you!"

For the numerous conference participants who sat through the rubber chicken banquet dinners and listened to my guest-speaker presentation of the journey, only to come up afterward and say, 'That was great—you should write a book,' I say "Thank you!" Here it is; enjoy it!

Thank you to my co-workers at the University of Minnesota, especially Phyllis Bakka, John Blanchard, Carrie Pike, and Jim Warren who thanklessly became test readers. I appreciate your honest feedback, editing comments that cleared up my verbal wanderings, and above all, your sincere encouragement to keep writing. To Bob Stine, thanks for all your support. I have been blessed to have you as a supervisor.

## Acknowledgements

A very special thanks to Kathleen Preece. Your talent and professionalism as an editor continue to make my writings better. Your great sense of humor and zest for adventure are matched only by your editing skills. I can imagine no other person better-suited to work with on a story of this nature than you. Please keep doing what you do so well.

Every now and then as we travel through life, we encounter people who have an aura of gentleness and trust. More times than not, we're not looking for it; it is just there. The first time I approached publisher Norton Stillman to discuss developing this book, I felt it. Any concerns I may have had about meeting to consider publishing One Good Story were immediately lost in our introductions. His patient, step-by-step guidance in the development process, his eye for layout, and his expertise in design were invaluable.

Most of all, this book is the result of one of the most loving, caring, and tolerant people who ever stood teary-eyed on a riverbank—my wife, Lila. Although her fears for my safety existed, she never allowed them to discourage my plans. Her love for me and her understanding of my need to heed the call of a river journey were always felt.

*To Lila*

# Table of Contents

*There's many a man who never tells his adventures,*
*for he can't hope to be believed.*
*Who's to blame them?*
*for this will seem a bit of a dream to ourselves in a month or two.*

SIR ARTHUR CONAN DOYLE

# Foreword

"HERE, 1,475 FEET ABOVE THE OCEAN, THE MIGHTY MIS-
SISSIPPI RIVER BEGINS TO FLOW ON ITS WINDING WAY 2,552
MILES TO THE GULF OF MEXICO."

*The informational words routered into a tree turn on the shore
of northern Minnesota's Lake Itasca, gave the facts of the big
river, accurately describing its origin. I couldn't help but wonder what other "facts" were missing about that river's long and
meandering journey to where it poured itself out into the Gulf.
I was about to find out.*

When I walked into the cafe early on the June morning, the tra-
vails of my travel were undoubtedly quite evident. Hair only
"somewhat" combed without the assistance of a mirror; cutoff jeans that had seen many miles on the seat of a kayak; hands
and face bearing the leathery look of one in the sun and the
wind, perhaps a day too long.

My waitress's quick smile and warm welcome were unexpected. And the coffee especially embracing. "Where you coming from," was all she had to ask before I found myself, once
again, caught in the graces of river travel, and I began to unfold
my story for her. She listened, served my breakfast, left my bill,
then went on to other tables with a quiet and sincere: "That's
one good story."

The call of the river had come early in life to my ears and to
my soul. In 1959, my parents moved to East Peoria, Illinois to

manage a boat marina on the Illinois River. I was nine-years-old at the time and had no idea of the effect that riverside up-bringing would have on the rest of my life.

It was not long before my brother and I saved enough money to buy a small, plywood boat and outboard motor. That 10-foot craft became our license to take on the roles of a modern-day Tom Sawyer and Huck Finn. Much to the concern of our parents, our summer days were spent exploring the Illinois River, going as far around each 'next bend' as the old 15-horse Evinrude and five gallons of gas would take us.

It was no surprise when I visited the Headwaters nearly a decade later, I could feel the bite of that childhood river-adventure bug. I recall saying during that visit (to my not-yet-known-to-be future wife, Lila): 'Wouldn't it be great to put a boat in here at the Headwaters and go all the way to the Gulf?' I don't recall her reply, but the thought never escaped me and the passing years only heightened the infection.

Nearly 25 years later, I found myself standing on the same bank and reading that same sign. Things had changed—the young girlfriend had been my wife of nearly a quarter century, and this time I had come to the banks to cure the infection—a 2,552 mile river trip from the Mississippi's orign at Lake Itasca, Minnesota, to the Gulf of Mexico.

The decision was made to do the trip solo, and in a one-person, 17-foot kayak. There were several reasons that travel-ing solo was the right way to do this river. Although I had of-fers from friends to help canoe the river, most were only able to take limited amounts of time off and no one could accompany me on the entire journey. Because of the difficulty of paddling a canoe by myself against winds that can blow mightily across some of the river's bigger waters, I decided the most efficient craft would be the solo sea kayak. Fortunately, my neighbor had such a craft; he graciously offered it to me for the 2,552 mile journey.

The route was set, the craft lined up, yet one of the greatest challenges lie ahead—the packing of the kayak. This was an art that had to be repeated every morning of the journey. Eventually, an equation was developed: *Everything has a defined space, with accessibility proportional to its probability of daily use.*

For easy access the life jacket, rain coat, hat, maps, and water were held in place by elastic cargo netting in the immediate front deck. Behind the seat were the "secondary" essentials: suntan lotion, first-aid kit, and camera. The spray skirt was kept in my lap on the floor between my legs for quick access.

The paddle was permanently tethered with tough elastic cord to the front deck, and sleeping bag and maps were kept in a waterproof bag in the rear of the kayak. A one-person tent, sleeping pad, cook kit and stove, and extra water filled the rest of the stern.

Food was separated into three bags for their respective consumption: breakfast, lunch and supper, with all three courses stored in the narrow portion of the bow in front of the foot area. Bow and stern each had a molded inflated float bag to keep the durable plastic kayak from sinking should it fill with water.

The amount of planning that was invested in packing that kayak, was totally lacking in determining camping locations down the river as the journey progressed. There were too many variables in a day to determine "where" one might be when dusk settled. Slow currents and a head wind might mean only a 25-mile paddle. The only criteria for a campsite besides safety, was a flat spot in the terrain.

Not far into the journey, I became proficient at making that night's camp, with the process taking only 45 minutes. The routine went like this: boil water in the two-pound coffee can on the stove while setting up the tent and laying out the sleeping pad and bag. When the tent was up, the pasta was simmering, and the metal cup of water for coffee took its place on the stove.

Within 20 minutes my meal could be cooked and devoured; all that was left was to wash the coffee can cooking pot, store the metal cup and utensil in it, and seal it with its plastic lid. After a cooling dip in the river I turned in. It was a repetitive pattern—for 43 nights.

Preparation for the river adventure included only one major misconception. It had nothing to do with the speed of the winds I would encounter, the power of river currents, nor my own stamina to paddle a journey of this distance.

It had to do with people. When I took that first dip of the paddle at the Headwaters, I had convinced myself of the prudence of avoiding contact with people. My reasoning was sound (or so I was convinced). There was the chance of bodily harm and, of course, opportunity for theft by strangers. I could not have been more wrong.

The song, "Proud Mary," by Credence Clearwater Revival has a verse that says: 'The people on the river are happy to give.' And so they were. When I reminisce about the journey, it is the encounters with people I met that are my fondest. An outright smile, a willingness to share, a friendly hello—all were commonplace on the river. The river seemed to be no ones turf and all had equal rights to its passage. And river people all seemed to want to hear, one good story.

For whatever reason, I found people were happy to give. Should you ever begin to lose faith in the goodness of humanity, spend time on the river. You, too, will find one good story.

# ONE
# GOOD
# STORY

# Little
# Mississippi

## FIRST DAY

Lila handed me the baseball cap. The kayak was loaded, ready, and waiting. Check lists had been checked and rechecked. All that was left was to climb into that river craft and begin the journey. My spouse stood at my side while we looked over Lake Itasca, discussing once again how many days it would take me to reach the City of Brainerd in central Minnesota. There we would meet, go over equipment needs and make the necessary changes and/or deletions. That would be my last opportunity for such family support.

We had been over all of these details a number of times and we both knew it was a ploy to prevent, not the start of the trip—but the beginning of a time of separation and all the concerns that accompany being apart. It was, 'just another canoe trip,' I suggested, giving Lila a 'see-you-in-eight-days kiss,' and pushed off shore into the 12-foot wide Mississippi River, the swift and rippling 14-inch deep current carrying the kayak downstream.

The river is crystal clear and cold at its origin at Lake Itasca, becoming fickle its first few miles across the country. In one spot, the river is 6-foot wide and 3-foot deep; around the next bend, it's 20-feet wide and 6-inches deep.

And her challenges come in many shapes, speeds, and sizes. For some reason, I had not envisioned the existence of beaver dams on the Mississippi River. I thought of river barges and therefore, a big river. But beaver dams seemed more aligned with the small streams that meander the forested land of our state. In reality, beaver dams do exist on the Mississippi River—and lots of them. For the first two full days of paddling, barges became a distant thought and beaver dams the challenge of my hours.

Scaling beaver dams became an art on this journey to the Gulf. At the first few dams I encountered, I paddled up to the dam, carefully climbed out of the kayak, pulled it over the dam trying to find a spot below that would allow me to get the craft pointed down river.

This seemed like a reasonable approach. However, with each dam, the going was tricky and time-consuming and I found myself getting wetter and muddier than the time before. I seemed to have found a solution when, upon getting ready to scale a small dam, I saw it was only a two foot drop to the river on its back side.

"Hmm, white water and a kayak? Looks like a match to me," I said out loud. Paddling back up the river 20 yards I turned toward the spillway and began to paddle hard. The kayak shot easily over the dam and splashed into the water on the down river side. "Piece of cake!"

The procedure worked well for the next few dams until I reached one where the water was flowing freely through the dam, instead of over it. There was a nearly 3-foot drop down the back side.

I moved some of the bigger sticks to allow water to escape over the top and, hopefully, carry the kayak with it. I paddled back up the stream from the dam spillway, going a little further this time and then, turning the kayak toward the dam, began paddling fast and hard. I hit the dam at a good clip, and the unthinkable happened. The friction against the kayak, caused by the lack of sufficient water flowing over the top of dam, broke the crafts momentum. The bow dropped the 3- foot height and stuck in the gravel of the stream channel. The stern pointed skyward, leaving most of the center of the kayak suspended in mid-air. I instantly thrust one end of the paddle into the ground to steady myself and to keep from rolling.

My first thought? "I hope no one is watching!" My canoe buddies back home would have shown no mercy. At best, they would laugh and offer worthless advice. At worst, they would try throwing sticks to knock the paddle out from under me. It was one of those stories that would have been repeated at every canoe trip, at every campfire over the next 10 years.

Thankful to be alone, I tried to move the kayak forward by applying pressure with my body in gentle forward thrusts. Eventually, the current began washing away the gravel that was holding the bow and I began to feel some movement forward. It took 10 minutes to get the kayak down the back side of the dam. I finally made it to river level safe and dry. I elected to get out and haul the kayak over the next few dams I encountered.

After the first day of paddling, I was exhausted. Those 19-miles had been an obstacle course. And the day was not over when I pulled up on shore at dusk. The evening's camp turned out to be an abandoned dry-grass pasture. I set up the tent and began the process of making dinner. I pressurized the one-burner cook stove and lit it. The flame wouldn't adjust so I began inspecting the stove. Finding a lose connection, I tried tightening it without first shutting the stove down. Bad decision. Turning the connection the wrong way caused a small stream of gas to squirt out and became ignited. A stream of lighted gas was now spraying into the dry grass and lighting it like a torch.

The fire began spreading, propelled by a light evening breeze. Stomping out a line of fire that was heading toward the tent, I grabbed my cooking pot, ran the five yards to the river and scooped up a can full of water. I must have made close to a dozen trips to that natural hydrant before I was able to bring the flames under control.

This 'first day' had been an interesting one—tougher than I had expected and hopefully not the mold from which the days and miles ahead would be patterned.

On my map, the "little Mississippi" stretch between the Headwaters at Itasca and Bemidji turned out to be a kayak obstacle course designed by nature. The stream was blocked by fallen trees, plugged by beaver dams, and rendered nearly impassable by log jams. At one point, in an attempt to maneuver through one particular log jam, I became pinned against a log by a current that was being forced under some logs, This, in turn, created a surface current that formed a perpendicular chute in relation to the direction of the flow of the river.

The kayak became pinned hard against the log and the current was relentless in its intent to pull it down under the log jam. I couldn't reach the stream bottom with the paddle so I did not have the option of pushing myself.

There was a branch stub near the bow but I couldn't reach it with the shoulder of the paddle blade at a good enough angle to hook it and pull myself forward. Behind me, I found a branch stub sticking up about two-thirds of the paddle length away. There was just enough stub into which to lodge the paddle blade and create force by gently leaning back. My intent was to slowly move the kayak forward along the log for about three feet. This effort got me within reach of the branch stub near the bow. I could now reach it with the paddle blade shoulder at an angle to create enough leverage to pull and slowly inch the kayak forward.

Eventually, the pinning current became less against the log and more in line with it, allowing the kayak to become loose. The entire process seemed to have taken 15 to 20 minutes. It was good to be out of danger and moving down the river again.

The eleven mile paddle across Lake Winnibigoshish was the only time a compass was needed to determine a straight line and the shortest distance to a desired destination.

CROSSING WINNIE

Lake Winnibigoshish ("Winnie") west of Deer River is the widest body of water that has to be navigated when traveling the Mississippi. To get from one side of the lake to the other, 11 miles of open water must be crossed, and then another three to get to where the river exits the lake.

My plans that morning had been to get across "Winnie" by days end, make camp, and avoid thinking about the long paddle at the start of the next day. The day had begun breezy. I had hoped for some mercy from the winds since it had been quite an effort to cross the five-mile wide Cass Lake into a northeaster earlier in the day.

I didn't expect Winnie to be gentle with me, but I was not anticipating the three-foot waves that greeted me as I paddled out of the river on to the lake. There were no routes across or along that lake that protected me from that northeast wind, nor from the waves it sent rolling across those 11 miles of open water. The trip was done for the day.

My map showed a campsite a half mile north along the west shore. I decided to make that my goal and put the rain coat on over the spray skirt. The waves rolled along, sometimes over the bow and splashed the spray skirt causing the water to find its way through the rain coat and into my cloths.

It was too wet and dangerous to paddle parallel to the breaking wave so I decided my best move was to paddle far enough out into the lake to give me enough angle to turn and go with the waves back to shore and, if all went according to plan, close to the campground.

My tactic worked—until it came time to land the kayak. My plan was to hit shore, jump out in time to pull the opened up kayak onto high ground before the next wave broke over the stern and spilled water into the open cockpit. Timing truly is "everything." I caught a wave and paddled hard, gliding as far up on the beach as possible. Popping the spray skirt loose I scrambled to get out before the next wave rolled in. It was not meant to be. That next wave rolled over the stern and disappeared into the cockpit. Grabbing the side of the kayak, I heaved it further up the beach. It was now safe from the next wave, but there was plenty of water getting at whatever it could in the stern storage area.

Luckily, it was still early evening and, with a few hours of daylight left, I was able to set up the tent in hopes that the hard-blowing wind would dry it out.

After an early supper I sat on the bank watching those high rolling waves pound the beach. The long rest was appreciated, but punctuated by restless fears about how long that east wind would have me pinned down on this west shore. I had experienced winds in northern Minnesota that would blow hard for several days at a time. One hundred miles into the journey and I had hit a potentially major delay. Time was miles and I was on a schedule. If I wasn't paddling, I wasn't going down river.

The tent was dry and I crawled in early, hoping for a good night's sleep. The wind buffeted the tent most of the night, strong enough at times to awaken me and register its continued presence. By dawn, however, the wind had calmed, settling down to a navigable speed out of the southeast. Within 40 minutes I had cooked and eaten breakfast and was paddling south with the thought of using the south shoreline as shelter should the wind decide to pick up as the day went on.

A half-hour into the morning's paddle, the wind quieted and it seemed logical to head straight across the lake. I figured I could make it in three hours. Pointing the bow out, I was very aware that there would be no landmarks to guide me. Remembering a compass I had packed away in the miscellaneous gear pocket behind the seat, I set a bearing, hoping it would put me on the shortest route to the dam located at the north east corner of the lake. I strapped the compass to the deck in front of me and began paddling out across the lake. This was the first time on the trip that I had felt so alone. I was truly by myself with no one knowing where I was on this day, on this huge lake, at this particular time.

I should have known the big lake wasn't through with me yet. Before long, the shoreline disappeared in an ever-growing thickness of fog. I wondered if the weather was changing and I was coming into rain. I continued to follow the compass bearing and began to paddle harder, hoping to get to the other side before the rain came. I was paddling in a world of grey—like an eerie scene from the Outer Limits television show. The only sound was the paddle dipping into the water. Blindly following the compass, the next two hours were a surreal experience. Finally, a dark gray cloud bank that I first mistook as another storm, materialized as the tree line of the east shore. After three hours of paddling, I had reached Winnie's eastern shore.

I was back to the little river again and, more importantly—for the first time the general lay of the river was south toward the Gulf and not in the northerly or easterly directions it had been taking me until now.


BACK TO RIVER TRAVEL

A curtain of cattails filled in the narrow river, affording little opportunity for a panoramic view. It was like paddling a maze where the only thing to see were walls of cattails on each side and a clear blue sky above. One had no idea of location except that it was part of a 13-mile river maze between Cass County Highway #18 on the west and Cass County Highway #18 to the south. The community of Deer River existed at only some imaginable location to the north beyond the wall of cattails.

The river mapped out like worm tracks in a dried up mud puddle. There was no sense of where you were or where you needed to go—except downstream. The river meandered through a flat, several-mile wide flood plain mazed with old river channels and abandoned oxbows.

At each intersection, a decision had to be made. A bad one would lead to a dead-end oxbow or being forced to turn around by a shallow, grown-over old river channel. A good decision might find the kayak turned and paddling in nearly the same direction I had come.

All of the potentially bad decisions, except one, were averted by studying the river current at each of the trickier intersections. I had learned earlier on the river to pick my way through the nearly mile-wide shallow rice beds west of lake Winnibigoshish by studying the effect of the current on newly emerging vegetation. The current was slow in the broad shallow river lakes so the wind could force the grass-like surface vegetation to point in whatever direction the wind was blowing (making it confusing to determine the direction of the current.)

The trick was to study the vegetation growing on the bottom of the lake. Bottom vegetation is not influenced by surface wind direction and would always correctly identify the direction of the river current, thus leading me to its outlet.

I tried to apply this insight to the ways of rivers and their currents at each intersection where a decision needed to be made in the cattail maze. At 140 miles from the Headwaters, the river water was still clear enough to let me see nearly five feet to the bottom.

A new trick I had picked up in the maze was to also study how strongly bent the vegetation was to determine in which direction the stronger of the divided currents went. Reading the current at the tricky intersections slowed the paddling down, but it was worth it if it prevented heading a mile down a grown-over oxbow, only to have to turn around and paddle back.

The frustration of paddling and "getting nowhere" culminated at a bend in the river where I could see three 30-foot willow trees growing at water's edge. I had been getting close to them for the last 20 minutes. They had caught my attention because they were the only things on the floodplain that wasn't cattail. I was paddling in what I guessed to be a westerly direction. However, as I reached the trees the river made a sharp turn back east.

Checking out the trees as I passed, I had to smile at the old and new bird nests nestled in the trees' branches, thinking what choice, bird-nesting real-estate the trees must be out here in the middle of the sea of cattails. I continued easterly another 20 to 30 minutes before the river swung back to what I perceived to be a southwesterly direction. Twenty more minutes of paddling, some small changes in course direction, and I came around a bend only to spot another group of trees on the horizon.

"Wow, this place is turning into a forest," I satisfyingly chuckled to myself. As I got closer, however, I had the sinking feeling those three trees had the very same characteristics of the three I had seen nearly an hour earlier. I remained in denial and argued with the cattails on each side . . . 'no way are those the same trees I passed an hour ago.'

The unmistakably familiar bird nests forced me to accept the unacceptable. Slapping the water with the paddle I shouted,

"Damn, I will never get to the Gulf." The river had been cutting thin east to west swaths back and forth across the broad flat flood plain. My hopes of making rapid progress toward the Gulf had been trashed by three willow trees and some bird nests. I was really beginning to dislike cattails.

## A BIFFY BEDROOM

Coming around the bend I could see the Minnesota State Highway #200 bridge ahead. Since last night's camp at the Schoolcraft State Recreation Area, I had traversed the Pokegama and Grand Rapids' dams and paddled about 58 river miles through an off and on afternoon drizzle. I was tired—more than tired; I was exhausted, damp, and chilled.

My goal had been to reach a primitive rest area where Highway 200 crossed the river at the community of Jacobson. Familiar with the rest area, I knew it would be a good campsite, with the added amenity of a bar located a few hundred yards from the east side of the bridge. I could taste the hamburgers and beer before the bridge was in sight.

The riverbanks of that wayside rest were steep, so I floated under the bridge, pulled the kayak up underneath, and headed "barside." Hot coffee in lieu of a cold beer, two "specials" and I was feeling good. Ordering another bar special "to go" in anticipation of tomorrow's lunch, as well as a beer for an evening treat, I headed back to make camp. I was hoping the beer would help me sleep more soundly through the aches and pains of sore muscles that frequently caused me to wake up during the night. The unfinished beer led me back to the kayak where I stowed away the extra gyro sandwich, hopefully safe from the night critters.

Sitting under the bridge, I polished off the last of the beer and turned my attention to making camp. Grabbing the tent, sleeping bag and pad from the kayak, I headed to the wayside rest area to set up and get some sleep. The night air had a slight drizzle and I figured when I broke camp in the morning I would have to put the tent away wet. I stopped at the newly-made outdoor biffy. Holding the door open, I stood there for a moment, letting my eyes adjust to the darkness. As its interior dimensions began to materialize, I had the absurd thought that just maybe a guy could sleep in here?

I propped the door with the tent to let as much light in as possible so as to get a better look. "Yep, this will do." I laid down on what I hoped was a clean concrete floor to see if I fit. My head and feet just barely touched opposite ends.

Close enough. This will do. I was as matter-of-fact as if checking out an uptown rental apartment. The door opened inward so it took some effort to let in light and get the sleeping area laid out at the same time. I unfolded the tent halfway to make extra padding for my hip and shoulder area, laid the sleeping pad on top of it, rolled out the sleeping bag, and for a pillow, set down the folded, rubberized dry bag I store my change of clothes in.

I stretched out to check the roominess—I still fit. Before I melted into the sleeping bag I took one of my shoes and propped the door open. A little more air exchange wouldn't hurt. Lying there smiling, I couldn't help but wonder what a picture this would make.

Sometime during the night I was awakened by a car pulling into the rest area. It came to a stop, followed by the opening of car doors and the sound of voices. I had thought earlier before going to sleep that if someone tried to get in, I would simply say, "It's being used," in as gruff a voice as I could muster.

However, after a few moments the voices quieted, the car doors closed, and the car pulled out of the graveled parking area and shifted its ways down the highway.

I awoke the next morning feeling more rested than I had for the past several mornings. Breaking camp was a snap. Hot instant oatmeal, steaming coffee, and the barroom "special" left over from the evening before.

The rising, early morning river fog parted ever so gently to let the kayak pass on its Gulfward journey. That first hour of daylight on the river is what I wish heaven to be like, for I know what hell is: 2 o'clock in the afternoon, exhausted from nine hours of paddling, hungry, your body wet and cold from the rain, and your destination lying in the darkness, six more hours away.

If, as some say, life is preordained, then one is at times, never quite certain if being on a journey is a reward or a punishment.

# Dams
# and
# Locks

Ottertail Power Dam down river from Bemidji

OTTERTAIL POWER DAM
CASS LAKE DAM
WINNIBIGOSHISH DAM
POKEGAMA DAM
BLANDIN DAM

LOW WOODEN DAM

ORIGIN
LAKE ITASCA

GRAND RAPIDS

BRAINERD

POTLATCH DAM

LITTLE FALLS DAM

BLANCHARD DAM

SARTELL DAM

ST. CLOUD DAM

COON RAPIDS DAM

MINNEAPOLIS
ST. PAUL

MINNESOTA

There are 12 dams (not counting "natural" beaver dams) and 28 locks that block the flow of the Mississippi River from its origin at Lake Itasca to Alton, Illinois where the last lock, number 26, stands. The eight, non-locking dams are located on the first 500 miles of river north of Minneapolis; each must be portaged.

The first of the 28 locks and dams begins at Minneapolis. The first two locks—Upper and Lower St. Anthony Falls, are not numbered and there is no lock and dam number 23 on the river between numbers 22 and 24. The reason for this is that the 9-foot minimum water depth for barge operation was adequate between locks 22 and 24 so Lock and Dam 23 was never built.

Low Wooden Dam, located just nine miles down river from the Headwaters, is the first man made obstruction across the river, not counting the 5-foot diameter culvert that either has to be portaged or navigated through within the first half mile of river. I elected to float it while staying with the kayak and then lost track of my whereabouts shortly after crossing under the Highway 200 bridge. I was quite surprised when I came around a bend of 7-yard-wide river and found myself headed for Low Wooden Dam.

My initial plans had been to make the designated 50-yard portage around the west side. I had no clue as to how dangerous the structure was and did not want to risk spilling and getting everything wet this first day of the journey. However, it became obvious that my boat was going over the structure—and me with it.

As the bow reached out over the drop, I could see the structure was formed with stacked logs like a step-ladder effect. 'This isn't so bad,' I thought, as the bow dipped. I leaned back to lower the center of gravity, stabilizing the kayak as much as possible. The long narrow bow buried itself into the pool of water at the bottom of the 4-foot drop and was pushed forward by the force of the remainder of the boat and the current. Eventually the bow popped back up and the kayak settled flatly on the surface of the pool.

Shouting a loud 'eee haww,' I looked back at the structure that now seemed much larger from my viewpoint below than it had from the top. My first thrill, my first adrenaline rush. But these moments of elation were neutralized by my now more unsettled feelings that I had made my first misjudgment on this journey. I had completed only nine miles of river. What did the remaining 2,543 hold in store?

The next dam was the Ottertail Power Company Dam—eight miles east of Bemidji and two days and 71 miles down river. It proved to be an uneventful 200-yard portage around the grassy mowed landscape of the hydroelectric dam. The portage was a nice break from paddling but it felt good to be back in the swift water on the back side of the dam. The next three dams—Cass Lake, Lake Winnibigoshish, and Cohasset were also uneventful, with easy portages around.

The Blandin Dam at Grand Rapids was not quite so simple. With the Blandin Paper Company mill occupying one side of the river and high, steep, and rocky banks on the other, it was nearly a half mile before one could gain access to the water again. For this reason, Blandin offers a portage shuttle service to anyone traveling the river. They assist travelers through town and back on the river about a half mile below the dam. It was about an hour before two friendly mill workers showed up in a pickup truck to help me load and transport the kayak and gear down river to a landing. Their patience was appreciated as they allowed me to stop at a convenience store and buy a large lemonade and sandwich.

The next 178 miles of river were unchecked by any dams between Grand Rapids and Brainerd. Just north of Brainerd the Potlatch Dam required a 200-yard portage, while the dam 40 miles down river from there at Little Falls required a 325-yard walk around. The biggest challenge at Little Falls was trying to cross the busy, in-town highway with a kayak and gear.

Nine miles below Little Falls (and 390 miles from the start of the journey at the Headwaters) is the Blanchard Dam. It almost went on record as being the termination point of this trip. I reached the dam late in the afternoon. The day had been overcast, cool and drizzly and I was correspondingly damp, tired, and hungry. After pulling the kayak up over the 5-foot vertical bank, I took a rest, drank some water, and ate a fruit bar. Feeling better I strapped on the pack and began pulling the kayak across the wet grass along the 125-yard portage. Stopping at the top of the 60-foot high bank on the dams backside, I studied the rock revetment used to stabilize the bank. I would need to climb down those large rocks to get to the river. Deciding to leave the pack at the top and return for it after I had taken the kayak down, I took the bow rope in one hand and the side of the kayak in the other and slowly proceeded over the edge of the bank.

All was going well until a third of the way down when I slipped on the wet rocks, causing me to lose my hold on the craft. The slack in the bow rope wrapped around my hand, allowed the kayak to shoot forward, pulling me with it. There was no way I would let go of the rope, knowing that on its own, my little ship would slide down the rocks and be lost to the swift river current below the dam.

I bounced over several large rocks before lodging myself against one of the biggest ones. Laying there, I tested all body parts; several movements caused groans but all parts seemed to do what they were made for. I decided I needed a much different approach to getting the kayak down the remaining 40 feet of bank to the river. I pointed the stern toward the river and then by holding onto the bow rope, I let the kayak slide itself down the bank as I carefully stepped from rock to rock, controlling the speed of descent. Safely reaching bottom and securing the kayak, I turned back to scale the 60-foot hill for the pack that I had left at the top. As I continued down river, I knew there were parts of me that, later in the evening, were going to remind me of that nasty tumble.

The dams at Sartell, St. Cloud, and Coon Rapids had long portages around them, but were uneventful compared to the Blanchard Dam. The Coon Rapids Dam was the last before reaching the lock and dam system and barge traffic at Minneapolis. It was good to be done with the portaging, but I wasn't sure that trading it for barge traffic was the better deal. People along the upper part of the river had warned me of the dangers of barges.

View from inside the Lower St. Anthony Falls Lock. I35 bridge in the background.

## THE LOCKS

I reached the lock and dam of Upper St. Anthony Falls early in the morning. This was to be my first try at "locking through" which was, admittedly, a bit intimidating. I began looking for lock traffic signals. The traffic signal was supposed to be a pole with the traditional red, yellow and green signal lights. The locking through procedure rules on my river map stated that if the traffic signal light was red, the locks were in use and to stand clear and not to approach. If the light was yellow, approach the

lock cautiously and under full control. A green light indicated it was safe to enter the lock. No light meant the lock was not in use and one needed to approach the guide wall, find the signal device, and pull the signal cord.

I bobbed around in the lock entry looking for the traffic light. Since I couldn't see red, yellow or green anywhere, I assumed the locks must not be in use. Besides, I didn't hear any noise that sounded like a big boat on the other side of those big doors ahead of me.

In my search for the traffic light, I unknowingly passed by the signal cord located out on the end of the approach wall. So now I am bobbing around, down in front of the lock doors and hollering up toward the lock building.

"Hellloooo, anybody home?" After about 10 minutes of intermittent shouting, I heard voices. Seeing the top of a head along the concrete wall above me, I whistled as loud as I could. Pretty soon the head peered over and, after a pause, a man said with an inquisitive tone: "How long ya been down there?" Upon hearing me admit to my 15 minutes of confusion, he pointed out the signal rope at the end of the concrete guide wall. He told me if I paddled back out onto the entry he would open the lock gate to get me through.

When I was half way out of the lock entry, I saw the red traffic light come on and the lock doors begin to open. When the doors were nearly all the way open, the red light switched to yellow and I began to approach slowly, not really knowing what to expect. The doors opened completely, the light turned to green, and the lock attendant motioned me forward and to the shore side of the lock chamber. He lowered me a rope, instructing me to just hang onto it and not tie it to the boat. Nor was I to tie the boat to the recessed ladder. Doing either would have dangerous consequences when the water was lowered into the chamber. The rope was meant to hold my place in the lock while the water in the lock chamber was being lowered.

I followed his instructions to the letter. The doors on the up-river side of the lock I had just paddled through closed, and the water level began to drop. The Upper St. Anthony Lock has the largest water level drop of all locks on the river—nearly 43 feet.

As I slowly dropped in the chamber, it was exhilarating to realize they were running this entire locking-through process for one guy in one small kayak. When the water level stabilized, the doors on the down river side opened and soon the lock attendant sounded the depart signal. As I paddled out along the entry guide wall, I looked back and again thought, 'All that for me?' It sure beat portaging.

The entire procedure had taken about 20 minutes and allowed me to take a rest from paddling. This locking-through stuff was all right! Less than a half mile down river was the Lower St. Anthony Falls Lock and Dam, but this time I knew where the traffic light was located. It wasn't on so I began to believe this may be a lucky day. I paddled up to the guide wall but the signal rope looked kind of high up off the water. It turned out to be three feet out of reach. No matter how far I stretched I was still several feet away from reaching the end of the signal rope. I couldn't get enough friction by reaching up and pressing the paddle blade against the wall to pull it down and trigger the signal.

Like the previous lock, I was now bobbing around in the entryway, trying to think of what to do next. I figured that since whistling and shouting worked the last time, I may as well try it again. Just as I approached the lock doors a man appeared at the edge of the lock wall and acted as if he had been looking for me. Feeling like I had to explain myself, I shouted up: "Hi! I tried to use the signal rope, but it was too high for me to reach from the kayak." He shouted back down that he hadn't known the rope was unreachable and thanked me for bringing it to his attention. I assumed he had been looking for me and shouted back my question asking how he knew I was here. He replied that the Upper Locks had radioed that I had just cleared their lock and was headed this way. He said he had seen me earlier out near the entry but then lost sight of me and decided to come looking.

The lock-through process was identical to the previous one with the exception it took about 10 minutes longer because of the need to fill the chamber. Apparently the last boat through was also headed down river so the chamber was left empty in case the next boat through was headed up river. The entire procedure took just under 30 minutes but was still an intimidating feeling. The small kayak in that cavernous lock chamber had no resemblance to a massive and steady river barge.

I held tightly to the rope as the water began to stir and swirl. I figured if something were to go wrong, this rope was my ladder to safety. When the water level stabilized, the massive lock doors slowly swung open, emitting a creaking noise. Once out of the chamber and heading down river I looked back and thought, 'Two down, 26 more to go!' Locking-through proved to be a welcome opportunity for a break in paddling. It also gave me the sense that progress was being made on the journey, while actually having to do very little!

Ford Dam, or Lock and Dam #1 as it is often referred to on the navigational charts, is the first numbered dam on the river. It's located approximately six miles below the St. Anthony Falls Locks and between the twin cities of Minneapolis and St. Paul. This lock and dam was my awakening to the fact that locking-through was not always a half-hour procedure.

When I arrived at the lock, several recreational boats were waiting to lock-through to head down river. I could see the helm of a barge that was just exiting the lock and heading down river. Not only did it take time for the barge to clear the lock, a number of recreational craft were waiting to come up river. It took some time for the lower river boats to enter, get squared away in the lock and then for the chamber to fill to river level. Once the lock doors opened on the up river side, we all had to wait for the exiting boats to clear before those of us who were heading down river could enter.

I was, by far, the smallest, and the slowest—I entered the lock last. The captains of each of the four other boats in the lock with me held on to the rope lowered to them by the lock attendant. This time the exit was a bit more exciting. Locking rules indicate you are supposed to enter and exit the locks at a controlled rate. This was no problem for me, but this meant half throttle and the creation of maximum wake to other boat operators. By the time I reached the exit doors of the lock chamber, the large wakes from the four boats were bashing and crashing into one another, ricocheting from one concrete side wall to the other. It was quite a challenge to keep the kayak going straight down the entry chute.

The lock process had taken over an hour. Talking with lock attendants at each dam, I learned that recreational craft have the lowest priority at the gates. Top on the priority list were emergency craft, followed by the commercial craft. It didn't take me long to reflect on the fact that locking-through could be a two-hour process, In theory, this step in my journey could cause me to spend 40 to 50 hours, the equivalent of nearly four days of travel time, waiting to get through the 25 locks remaining I would encounter on this journey. The option of portaging became an important one.

Lock and Dam #2 at Hastings was 32 miles down river from the first dam. I knew it would be dark by the time I arrived and that, most likely, I would be unable to transit the locks in darkness. I opted to make camp near the lock and then try a short portage in the morning, shown on the river map that leads over the dam levy to some backwater that reconnected with the river.

I was up early, ate, packed, and paddling shortly after dawn. The portage would have been quicker than locking-through had I not stopped to camp for the night. Each lock and dam was now to become an analysis of time verses energy as it related to total miles for the day. When comparing options, I decided I would take a hard look at portaging if there were any barges in the vicinity of the locks. The lock-through held the advantage of providing a 1/2-hour rest, but any delays on this journey came at the cost of miles made in a day.

## MISSISSIPPI QUEEN

Approaching Lock and Dam #18, I could see a big river boat sitting high in the lock chamber, headed up river. This meant it would soon be coming out of the lock, perhaps by the time I got there. My goal for the day was to get through or around #18 and find a place to camp for the night. It was 7 P.M. and I was tired. The portage option didn't look good so I decided to lock-through. This would give me a chance to take a closer look at that big river boat.

Earlier in my journey I had been passed twice—once going up river and once down—by the impressive white, five-story river boat the "DELTA QUEEN." I had heard that the MISSISSIPPI QUEEN was even larger and suspected this might be the big craft. The boat in the lock was playing a loud calliope music and a crowd of people were lining the lock wall. As suspected, this was the Mississippi Queen.

Mississippi Queen making her way up up river.

She stood six stories high, counting the helm, painted bright white and red with high-crowned twin side-by-side smoke stacks behind the helm. It was impressive, sitting in that chamber. It was nearly an hour before the boat's whistle signaled it was getting ready to leave. I paddled out and placed myself strategically behind the entry wall and between it and the shore line. I wasn't sure what kind of disturbance a huge boat like the Queen would create.

She emerged slowly, its calliope still playing, As it passed by the people on the boat waved from all levels. They were in a festive mood and as interested in me and my miniature craft as I was with them and the giant craft floating on the water, seemingly only a short distance away.

There was little disturbance around the lock entry and I waited in awe, dwarfed, as the river boat passed. Mounted on the side of the boat along the second deck were the huge red letters spelling the name, MISSISSIPPI QUEEN. So large were those letters, I presumed that the name could be read from either shore of the river as the boat passed by. And everyone on the river seemed to know when the Queen was passing. The entire five stories at the stern were surrounded by glass and brightly lit. The huge, twin red paddle wheels at the rear of the boat were churning and splashing water as they took the Queen up river. I wasn't sure if those paddle wheels were functional or decor, but the sound they made as they worked the water was the exact sound I would have expected a great paddle wheeler to make. I was caught in another era as I paddled out into the entry of the lock.

I hadn't expected my own passage to be quite so noteworthy, but the crowd that gathered for the passing of the Mississippi Queen seem to find as much interest in my own travels. As the signal light turned green, I headed toward the lock. Paddling into the entry, I could see people pointing toward me and having animated discussion with their neighbors. As I entered the lock chamber, someone began clapping until most of the crowd was cheering me as I headed toward the lowered rope near the center of the chamber.

Smiling and laughing, I answered the first question, 'Where are you from?' with a theatrical tired, pointing motion: "A thousand miles back that way." I paused for effect and continued: "The beginning of the river at Lake Itasca in Minnesota."

A barrage of questions came floating down: "How many days have you been paddling? Where are you going? How long will the trip take? Where do you sleep? eat? Have you ever tipped over?"

I answered questions as the water level began to drop in the lock. I hadn't even noticed that the lock doors had shut. Hanging onto the rope and floating in place, it was 15 minutes of rapid-fire question and answer time. Before I knew it, the lock doors were opening. Easing away from the wall I answered a few more questions then indicated it was getting late and I had to be finding a place to camp for the night.

As I began paddling the remaining crowd again began to applaud, shouting "good luck" and "safe travel" wishes. The interaction with the crowd had felt good. The isolation of being out on a river, and being out there alone is a battle of the mind that one encounters daily. Any opportunity for interaction with people was becoming a desirable detail of any day.

In the end, the batting average for locking-through versus portaging was about 500. The last lock, Lock #26 located at Alton, Illinois, 15 river miles above the St. Louis Missouri, was the newest, largest, and busiest lock on the river. It had replaced old #26 that had been built in the 1930s.

This was the last lock—it seemed prudent to portage around its west side when I climbed up the embankment on the locks west side and surveyed the up and down river traffic. Barges were locking through and barges were backed up to do the same. Portaging was a good decision.

Behind the levy was a large mud flat between me and the river. Surveying the flats and laying out what seemed like the easiest route across that mud, I zig-zagged my way, trying to stay on the drier, crusted mud surface. In a few places the crust stopped. I wasn't' about to backtrack so I plodded and slipped out across the semi-soft mud. Mississippi mud is the stickiest, slipperiest, and dirtiest substance on this planet. Once I reached river's edge I cleaned the mud off my shoes and kayak, repacked and, with a great sense of relief and accomplishment thought to myself: "Forty dams and locks. Well done."

# People on
# the River

Taking a mid morning break I visited with two commercial fishermen cleaning the mornings catch at a cleaning table on the river bank near Guttenberg, Iowa. Several species of fish they were cleaning I had never seen before. One species had a prehistoric appearance. The fishermen identified it as a shovel nose sturgeon, indicating it was very good eating. I was offered a meal of fresh fish filets, but had to decline the offer since I had no way of cooking the fish.

Two fellow kayakers from Japan were also on journey down the Missis-sippi River heading for St. Louis, Missouri. The two happy-go-lucky paddlers were students at the University of Missouri—Columbia. We had camped only a half mile apart the night before, missing a grand op-portunity to have camped together and talk.

They had begun their journey at Minneapolis, three days earlier, which surprised and disappointed me, for I had come through Minneapolis just the day before and had paddled in one day what had taken them three days to do. Meaning, I wouldn't be spending much time with them if I was going to make any kind of distance this day. Their slow pace was understandable when a barge approached and they retreated to the shore pulling their kayaks up on shore with them. I followed along just to use the shore time to break and talk with them while the barge past. They seemed a bit in awe and maybe a bit of disbelief when I explained that I never exit the river when a barge approaches—that it is quite safe to ride the swells out on the river away from the breaking waves near the shore line. After the barge past we returned to the river and paddled together for about a half hour before we said goodbyes. I pulled away leaving with smiles, safe journey wishes and raised paddle salutes for each other. I never learned if they succeeded in making it all the way to St. Louis, Missouri.

Clamming could be a very dangerous but lucrative business on the river. The pools above lock and dam numbers 9, 10 and 11 had the richest clam beds. Mostly, the clammers worked in teams of two. One person remained in the boat hoisting the clam bag when it was filled by the person feeling their way along the black river bottom. When the bag was full, the person on the bottom of the river would pull the signal rope attached to the bag and the person in the boat would raise the heavy bag using a boom mounted in the boat. The person in the boat empties the bag into the boat and then sends the bag back down to be refilled. The person in the boat then separates the empty clams and sorts the live clams by species and size while all the time keeping a watchful eye for approaching barges. If a barge approached the person on the bottom would be signaled by the same rope used for raising the clam bag. The bottom person would surface and they would move a safe distance from the oncoming barge.

A good clamming day could bring in $500 to $1000 for each person. All clammers would keep a sharp eye out for disfigured clam shells. Disfigured clams or "crippled" clams, as some clammers called them, were indications that a fresh water pearl was present in the clam. Finding a quality pearl would be a very special monetary bonus for the day. One crew of clammers told of a fellow clammer who, earlier in the season, found a sizable high quality, rose colored pearl in one of the clams and received $7,000 for it. They were also quick to point out that quality freshwater pearls of that value are rare.

Near Greenville, Mississippi I was paddling in the middle of the mile-wide river to take advantage of the swifter current when a fishing boat a half mile away on the Mississippi side of the river turned and headed out toward me. I watched carefully as it came directly at me. I was really hoping they were just coming out for "the story". The three guys in the boat were amazed that I was out on the river alone and had come so far safely. As it turned out one of the boaters, John Gwaltney, was president of Forestry Suppliers, a forestry equipment supplier I had a work account with for over twenty years. Since it was late afternoon and they were headed back from fishing, they emptied their cooler giving me a good supply of fresh fruit, tomatoes and onion buns. A month later I was to meet up with John at a forestry conference in San Francisco, California where he once again provided a good meal in return for a good story. Small world.

In need of drinking water the map indicated a town about a mile on the other side of the levee. I pulled the kayak up on shore and hid it in the brush and weeds. Hiding it was probably not necessary since I hadn't seen a soul all morning, with the exception of a few passing barges. I had also come to know that river people are very honest, at least those I had come in contact with and had a opportunity to share a story or two with. They seem to understand that everything I had was a necessity and important to my success and survival on the journey and were very respectful of it. Strangers on shore would offer to watch over my gear while I disappeared around a portage, over a levee or down a road to get drinking water or replenish supplies for the journey. At the beginning I was very apprehensive about leaving the kayak and all I owned behind. Somewhere around mid journey I began to sense that by asking people for their assistance they became a part of the journey and in some small way responsible for its' success and also enabled them to tell "one good story" at the end of the day.

Having no one around this particular time to entrust the kayak to during my foray into town, I figured better safe than sorry. I topped the levee and stepped onto the dirt road that the map indicated was there. About two hundred yards up the levee the road turned leading off the levee and into town. As I approached town I would wave at those who would look at me as they drove by. Almost no one would wave back or even acknowledge my presence. The response was predicable, it had happened nearly every time I had left the river and gone into a town. I know the response was in part due to my usual scruffy appearance from being on journey and the lack of opportunity to associate me with the kayak and river travel that caused the avoidance, yet I was always intrigued by the difference in friendliness between people on the river and people away from the river.

River recreationists could be found all along the river and were a great source for communicating back to my wife where I was, that I was ok and still talking somewhat coherently. People who worked on the river were equally as friendly and helpful as the recreationists. The lock attendants, barge workers, commercial fishermen, clammers, all were equally interested in the journey and willing to assist if needed.

Out of all the friendly people whom I encountered on the journey I have yet to meet any of them again, with the exception of one—John Gwaltney. I often wonder if any of them have one good story about the time they met this guy who was paddling down the Mississippi.

## TOONERS

When 10 hours of river lies ahead of a guy when he breaks camp at dawn, he can get to feeling that he is the only one on the river, but he's not. There are "tooners," out there.

It was a mid-Sunday afternoon when I paddled into a pool of water just above the Coon Rapids Dam near the town of that same name in Minnesota. "Pool" is the term used for describing the body of water held back by each dam on the river. The dam is the last on the Mississippi before reaching Minneapolis and the start of the river barge traffic. I was anticipating one last routine day before having to dodge the big boats for the remainder of the trip down river.

It was sunny and warm; the kind of day that makes paddling the only thing to be doing. Pleasure craft traffic had been moderate and all of the folks were considerate, slowing and keeping their distances when we passed one another. At the point where the Rum River meets the Mississippi however, the boat traffic steadily increased and there was less than respect for my slower moving craft.

When I reached the widest part of the pool, about three miles above the dam, there were more boats—of more sizes and shapes—than I had seen in total so far on the trip. I ventured a guess that every citizen in Coon Rapids was occupying this watery space. The water's surface was a froth of non-directional wave chop caused by boats going in every conceivable direction. I bobbed in place a short while, watching the show and wondering how any of that could be thought of as relaxing recreation. That is, all except the "tooners." These were the folks in the pontoon boats and they seemed to own the patent on the "pleasure."

Some of the tooners were slowly "putzing" up or down the river; others were tied two or three together, creating the likes of a floating party barge. Each seemed to be in slow motion and unconcerned with the mix of jet skis, speed boats, and ski boats zipping by.

It was a warm, mid-afternoon by now and I was thirsty and ready for a break. About a hundred yards ahead two pontoons were tied together. I picked a line of travel that would discreetly take me close to them, without looking like it was an intentional visit. I discovered I had a penchant for seeking opportunities for a beverage and, ultimately a snack!

The nine people on the two boats were watching me and exchanged smiles and waves. As I began to pass, one shouted, 'Where 'ya headed?' I replied: "Gulf of Mexico." Bingo! Someone else shouted and waved for me to paddle closer. I changed direction with a subtle effort as if I were doing them a favor by interrupting my journey to visit with them. Smiling all the way, I paddled over. I had learned that the easiest way to pop open a cooler lid was a friendly smile. I have to admit, I enjoyed these encounters as much, if not more than the people I met did. I can talk and drink at the same time!

As always, the barrage of questions ensued: 'Where did you start? How long will it take? How can you sit in a kayak all day?'

I answered with the standard replies and, with a somewhat less than enthusiastic voice, shared the fact that 'most of my food is dried and I drink mostly water because that is what I have the most access to.' Such a pathetic response elicited the offer of a can of pop, and then another. When a candy bar was added, the answers to questions were obviously made with improved humor on my part!

I had a few questions of my own regarding their floating tandem situation. They said they do this float thing frequently and sometimes have as many as six tooners tied together. The term "tooners" was the term used to separate themselves from "speed freaks" and other boaters. A bit more story trading and I headed out, turning the bow down river.

My pleasurable encounter with river drifting tooners was short-lived, however. I was paddling about 40 yards out from shore to stay away from the Evinrude zoo in the middle of the pool when I spotted a boat pulling a water skier coming directly at me. I stopped paddling, knowing I didn't have time to move to shore and get out of their way.

It was obvious they saw me and it appeared that the skier's intention was to pass on one side of me, while the boat towing him was going to pass on the other side. If this was the case, I wanted to be facing the rope head on and not get caught broad side trying to get to shore. I didn't know if they were just having some fun and wanted to pass the rope over me, or if they were going to try and throw me from the kayak by lowering the ski rope as they passed.

I quickly placed the flat side of my paddle blade under the cargo strap on the deck in front of me, hoping the strap would hold the paddle down and prevent the ski rope from getting under it and catching me about the chest—conceivably pulling me from the kayak or tipping me over. If successful, the rope would ride up over the paddle with the other end of the paddle resting on my shoulder; my head bent down below shoulder level.

Hoping skinned knuckles would be the worst of it, I was getting ready to duck when I saw the skier lift the rope high. He was smiling; I was not. But his smile and facial expression signaled fun and not danger. The rope passed high above me and they continued up river. As fast as the perceived danger had appeared, it disappeared.

This was the first physical threat I had encountered on my journey thus far. Unfortunately, it created questions in my mind about what other "people encounters" might lie ahead. I tried not to dwell on this, but found myself paddling only 20 yards from shore and feeling an uncomfortable distrust and increased sense of caution on the river.

I hadn't gone far before I passed another pontoon anchored near shore. An older couple was fishing and, when I passed, the gentleman asked 'what was that all about?' He had witnessed the skier episode. He made a comment about all kinds of people on the water and asked if I was all right, and if a beer might help.

Knowing a question and answer session, topped off by a cold beer would help take my mind off the unsettling event, I drank the beer and talked river with him. Refusing a second beer, knowing that a two-beer/kayak mix wasn't safe, I took the old man up on the offer to pack it and drink it later. His wife handed me two homemade brownies and I could only add that they were well-frosted with my own smile as I continued my down river paddle.

## LARRY THE IDIOT

I had two hours before dark and, looking at the map and gauging how far down river I might get, I figured I could make another 6 miles and reach a place the map identified as North Mississippi Park. Parks along the river had proven to be very nice places to camp, having the amenities a river traveler appreciates at the end of the day—drinking water, latrines, sometimes shower facilities, and always a nice, soft, level, grassy spot to pitch the tent. The latter was becoming more and more appreciated after many nights of camping on river banks that were far from level. A person just can't get a good night's rest on uneven ground.

The last two miles of river cut a path through a heavily urbanized and industrialized area. I was beginning to think I was going to be a lot closer to downtown Minneapolis than I would be comfortable with. As I approached the landing area, it became obvious this was not a typical river park. The park seemed to consist only of a blacktop parking lot, boat ramp, a couple portable toilets chained and padlocked to anchor bolts, and gang graffiti everywhere.

The paths in the wooded areas were trampled hard and bare. Bicycle skeletons and auto parts were strewn everywhere. I walked back to the kayak, tired and hungry and uncertain what to do.

The opposite bank looked no more inviting and it was getting too late to travel further. Anyway, the locks would be closed to pleasure craft this late in the evening. A couple islands about a half-mile back up river seemed to be my safest bet. I had passed them up as potential camping locations, anticipating all the amenities I was sure to find at the park. As I stood there, indecisive and too tired to move, I noticed a man in his late twenties, fiddling around with his boat at the other end of the boat ramp. He approached me and asked if I was planning to camp here. When I shared my reluctance with him to do so, he said matter-of-factly, "I live around here and believe me, you don't want to be here after dark."

He introduced himself only as "Larry," and I returned the greeting with, "Ron." We made the usual rounds of questions and answers and then he suggested I jump in his boat and let him haul me and the kayak up river to the first island. It was a great offer, which I gladly accepted, but with some caution. Larry appeared friendly, but he seemed to be a half step behind in our on-going conversation. We prepared the boats, meanwhile discussing the river, wildlife, the natural environment and all the ecological changes I had seen along its banks. After a bit, Larry asked what I did for a living. When I said I was a forester and that I grew trees for a living he perked up and said, "Oh yea! That's wild. I grow things, too." When I asked if it were fruits and vegetables, he responded with a "no," that it was "natural things."

I was too tired to play a question and answer game so I just nodded and let the conversation drop. Tying the 10-foot tow rope, to which my kayak was fastened, to the back of Larry's 16-foot fishing boat. I got into the middle of Larry's boat and pushed off from shore. Larry began idling away while handing me a beer.

His boat was a mess—plastic flower pots scattered around, a pile of burlap bags in the bow, and black dirt all over the floor. I thought it was odd, but surmised that he comes to the river to get rich silt soil for his herb growing.

The kayak being towed actually held the greater share of my attention. When I was comfortable that it was towing well, I gave Larry the nod to increase speed. We had only traveled a short distance when the little craft began darting back and forth behind the fishing boat like a zig-zagging fishing lure on a line. I hollered for Larry to stop the 15-horse power Johnson outboard. I untied the tow rope and pulled the kayak up along side, tying it near-even with the bow of Larry's boat.

We tried it again and this time things seemed to be working fine. Larry began to increase the speed; at half-throttle I hollered "good enough." The bow wake from the boat was just missing the bow of the kayak and the strength I needed to stabilize the kayak was challenging, but comfortable for the distance we had to travel.

I don't know if Larry didn't hear me or he chose to ignore me, but he cranked the throttle wide open. The wake from the bow came up over the kayak, collapsing the spray skirt that covered the seat compartment, instantly filling the kayak with water and sinking it with all my gear in it.

The instant I saw what was happening, I angrily shouted,

"Stop, you idiot." I am not sure if he even heard me but the commotion ended as quickly as it had started. I was not only tired and hungry, I was mad. It was obvious; Larry began apologizing, indicating he had no idea that this would happen. I calmed down when the kayak floated back to the surface and stabilized, still mostly submerged. We headed toward the west bank of the river.

Larry continued to apologize as he helped pull the kayak on shore. He was sincerely sorry and I began to feel badly for calling him names. My biggest concern turned to my 35 mm Minolta camera. The rest of the gear was packed in dry bags or could easily be dried out. The camera was a different story. Sometimes on warm days I open the camera bag to ensure that moisture doesn't develop. I wasn't sure if the bag was open or closed from my travels earlier in the day. Locating the bag, I breathed a sigh of relief to find I had closed it the last time I had used it. The camera had stayed dry in the water-filled kayak. I was calmer now. Without unpacking the little craft we turned it over and let the water drain out. In a matter of minutes we were back on the river and headed toward the island—this time at a slower pace.

When we reached the new camp, dusk was approaching and Larry's offer to help me set up camp was appreciated. After helping pitch the tent, Larry got a couple more beers out, sat on a nearby log and talked idly while I cooked my Lipton chicken and rice dinner. He declined my offer to share the meal, brought out another round of beer and commented that he had never seen anyone on his island.

I asked him where "his" island was and he hesitantly told me it wasn't far from here. When I asked what he did on his island he replied that he just "grew" things on it. Suddenly, it all came together: the burlap bags, flower pots, dirt on the floor of

Island Campsite

the boat, growing natural things and secret islands. Ole' Larry boy was farming some illegal plant on one of these islands. Maybe this one!

I instantly conjured up images of drug enforcement officers bursting out of the brush, storming the camp, and arresting me as an accomplice to Larry the Idiot. Getting control of my imagination was difficult but I realized that the scenario probably had a slim chance of happening. Besides, I could prove I was just an innocent adventurer on a journey, couldn't I? I had lots of maps, a kayak, camping gear, a wet tent, and three-days growth of beard to substantiate my story. On the other hand, maybe Larry was only growing natural condiment herbs? Yeah, right!

With a full stomach, the concern of where to camp alleviated, and three really good tasting beers in me, I was getting relaxed. While listening for the D.E.A. agents rustling in the bushes, I continued my conversation with Larry about life in general. I think he must have been testing those herbs earlier. The city lights were serenely reflecting off the water and the pauses between conversations were getting longer. Larry finally said he should probably be heading back to the landing before someone stole the wheels off his car. Anyway, we were out of beer. As he got up to leave he asked if there was anything I needed.

"Can't think of anything, but thanks for the offer," I replied. He asked how I was doing for money. I told him a guy doesn't need much on the river, He reached into his pocket and pulled out several coins and handed them to me. He seemed to want to help me with the journey, or he was still feeling bad about the boat incident.

"It's just chump change," he said. "Buy yourself a good cup of coffee in the morning. There is a 24-hour convenience store on the east bank of the Lowery Avenue Bridge crossing."

I reached out, shook his hand, and thanked him for the hospitality. We exchanged good-byes and best wishes and he turned, gave his boat a push out from the beach and jumped in. He drifted a bit and then, without looking back, started the motor and headed down river, disappearing into the shimmering river lights.

I stood at the water's edge for a while, listening to the noise of the motor fade as he headed down river. In moments it was quiet and I was alone again. I thought, 'what an evening, what a character,' and what a good night's sleep I was going to have after drinking those beers. I rolled out the dry sleeping bag on my unlevel bed and went to sleep analyzing the generosity of the people on the river—and half listening for the drug agents in the bushes.

## AQUAHOLICS

I was paddling around the last bend of the river before it entered Spring Lake—a two-mile wide pool of water created by Lock and Dam #2 at Hastings, Minnesota. It was late afternoon—about the time a cold drink and a hot supper fills one's fantasies. Just ahead on a large sand dune I could see two sharp looking speed boats tied to shore, a couple large tents set up, and four people stretched out on chaise lounge lawn chairs in the sand.

Now this looked like a cold-pop spot with a high potential relaxation opportunity. I started paddling a little closer without looking real obvious, but close enough for talking distance as I passed their camp. They were all watching me so I gave a distinct wave and a grin and resumed paddling. All four waved back—two men and two women. One of the men finally yelled out the standard distance question and I hollered back, "To the end of the river." But, following my instinctive nature that sometimes earns me a cold drink and a meal, I answered just low enough to be barely audible. He cupped his hand behind his ear, indicating he couldn't hear me very well and motioned for me to come closer. That was the signal I was hoping for.

I paddled past the two boats tethered to shore and read their names: "Aquaholics" and "Wet Dream." I grinned, thinking these were some fun-loving people. The guy who had called out, who I later learned was Dave, got out of his chair and came to greet me. Soon the other three joined, introducing themselves as Janet, Rick, and Evelyn. Rick asked if I would like a pop, saying he would offer a beer but they had only two left. A pop would be great, I said, admitting that the kayak is too tipsy for me to be drinking beer this late in the day in my attempt to take the awkwardness out of his offer.

We moved up toward the campfire; Dave handed me the pop and pointed to a cooler to sit on. I had no sooner said thanks and sat down when Dave's wife, Janet, offered a hamburger on the grill, leftover from their supper. My face must have showed my delight because the hamburger was accompanied by a large helping of potato salad, bean salad, and cole slaw. I tried to answer questions amid bites. The meal was delicious and hopefully my "thanks" was as hearty as my appetite had been. It was the best and largest meal I'd had in days and certainly had saved me from another heat and eat Lipton noodle meal.

I learned that the four of them were from Winona, Minnesota and were on the river recreating nearly every weekend during the summer. This particular time they were on a four-day, 260-mile round trip up to Minneapolis and back. This was their first day on the river and they were spending the night on the dune. I had never been through Winona, but would be paddling through Lock and Dam #5 at that location in about two days.

Dave asked if I knew where in Minneapolis they could replenish their beer supply. I wasn't sure, but I knew the location of an easy-to-get-to convenience store near the Lowery Avenue Bridge. It might carry beer. I had another nine miles to go down river where I was hoping to camp in the area near Lock and Dam #2 at Hastings, so I thanked them for their generous hospitality and we exchanged goodbyes. I jokingly suggested that if they passed me on their way back to Winona, "toss me a beer." They said they would be looking for me!

I made camp at Hastings that evening and the following night at a park in Lake City after an exhausting windy, late afternoon of paddling on the Lake Pepin stretch of river. The Lake Pepin stretch is two miles wide and nearly 20 miles long. It's extremely slow paddling on windy days.

I approached Lock and Dam #5 at Winona early afternoon of the next day. A barge traveling upriver had just cleared the locks and several pleasure craft that were heading down river were already entering to lock through. I paddled hard to beat the closing of the gates so that I could make the passage through with the rest of the boats. I was the last one in and they closed the gates behind me. I paddled over to grab the mooring line the lock attendant had tossed down for me to hold on to. It was a welcomed rest after that race to make it into the lock.

The water level began to drop when I heard a voice above me shout "Hey you!" It was the lock attendant, standing 15 feet above me. He said, "Miller time," and held a beer out over the railing, indicating he was going to drop it down to me. With a puzzled look, I held out my hands to catch it. "Nice catch," he hollered.

This was great—the Corp of Engineers was now serving beer to boaters that passed through. But then I learned who my real hosts were. The attendant hollered down that the beer was from the people up ahead in a boat named Aquaholic. He said they had told him that I deserved the beer. I jockeyed the kayak to see down the line of boats and there, about four boats up, were Dave and Janet in Aquaholic and Rick and Evelyn in Wet Dream. They were waving to me so I held the beer up in a thank you salute and resumed my place at the mooring line.

When the gates opened and the boats began to clear out of the lock, they held back for a moment to wish me luck on my journey and to bid a final farewell. They then headed down river and disappeared around the bend.

After I cleared the turbulence of the locks, I popped open the can and floated down river while I drank the beer. I was once again mindful of, and thankful for the generosity of the people on the river.

## THE SATISFIED FROG

Rounding the river bend nine miles below Lock and Dam #17, I was heading toward a large island in search of a place to camp. The Keithsburg lighted Day Marker on the east bank of the river identified my exact location. The island was almost directly across from the town of Keithsburg, Illinois, or so the map indicated. The levee hid everything that lie behind it from view, so I just assumed the town was there. The U.S Corp of Engineers-Upper Mississippi River Navigational Charts hadn't been wrong yet.

Approaching the island I wondered if I would have as much trouble finding a place to camp as I had the night before. Recent high water levels caused by heavy rains in Iowa and Illinois had left a fresh coating of mud over most of the low areas along the river.

I preferred the island camping. Their isolation offered a higher level of security during the night than a shoreline did. I always seemed to sleep a little better. As I paddled along the shoreline of the island, it became evident there were no dry sandy spots on which to make camp so I turned my attention to the levee on the east side of the river. I knew there would be mud-free camping on the levee, or at least on its far side.

So far I had paddled nearly 1,200 miles without any personal threats from people and I was beginning to feel that my anxiety at the beginning of the trip about interacting with strangers on the river was unwarranted. In fact, every encounter had been favorable. I had not met anyone who had not taken the time to stop and talk and/or offered me something in the way of food or beverage, along with a "good luck" wish.

Of course, all encounters had been during the daylight hours. Island camping still gave me the security I sought after dark. I paddled across the river, the current carrying me down river a little farther than I had initially shot for. It was late and I was too tired to battle the current back. I landed the kayak in a mixture of gravel and mud with large pieces of broken concrete sticking out and lying about on the shore. The wave action from wind and barges had washed the chunks of concrete clean of mud, making it a good place to land without getting muddy.

I pulled the craft completely out of the water, lodged it between two pieces of concrete, and unloaded my gear in two trips, carrying it to the top of the bank on a grassy, mud-free spot. About 50 yards upstream an older gentleman was fishing in a small inlet and two young boys were climbing around on the pilings. All seemed unconcerned about my presence.

Looking the other direction I saw a one-lane dirt road that came up over the levee. The road trailed down the bank a short distance further to a parking or turn-around area. This vehicle access sparked some concern, but the spot at which I was standing was grassy and level and I would be able to hear any cars that came over the levee during the night.

It was a nice spot; I decided to risk it. My risk evaluation was based on my faith in the niceness of small-town people and the fact there was not any gang graffiti painted anywhere. I went down and grabbed the kayak, pulling it to the camping spot.

I set up camp and headed over to talk to the older gentleman still fishing by the little bay. The two young boys had left earlier on their bicycles. The old man didn't acknowledge my approach until I was nearly to him. He nodded a 'hi' to which I responded that it "looks like it will be a nice night."

He concurred and, after a bit more small talk on my part, said he'd watched me paddle across the river and cross over to this side. He questioned, in a grandfatherly way, the safety and wisdom of being on the river in that small boat. I assured him it was a safe way to travel as long as I was attentive to the dangers of the river.

He began the standard journey questions which, by now, I had canned answers for and could answer clearly and concisely. I was becoming an efficient communicator when it came to questions about the journey.

When there came to a break in the conversation, I asked if he was from around the area. He said he was born and raised in the Keithsburg area. I pondered this because earlier he had asked where the river began and now I found it odd that someone who had spent his whole life along that river had not made enough of an effort to learn its origin.

I had encountered similar situations several times and, each time, found it perplexing. I questioned him as to the safety of my camping spot and he reassured me it was the "safest place on earth." Upon further questioning, he informed me that town was a short distance on the other side of the levee and added, "It's not much of a town, only about 700 people or so."

When questioned about a breakfast spot for morning, he pointed to the road over the levee and said to go two blocks past the edge of town, take a right, and look for a cafe on the left side of the street. We exchanged a few more comments and I headed back to camp. We never did exchange names which I guess are not always necessary.

At camp I took out the stove and cooking can, and the treat-of-the night—Lipton Spanish rice dinner. I was boiling supper but I was sure looking forward to breakfast. Sitting on the bow of the kayak I ate the rice as I gazed out over the river. The evening sky was pale pink and clear and the water calm except for little ripples caused by the gentle current. Truly, it was a beautiful evening on the river. Even after having paddled nearly

1,200 miles, the river at the end of each hard day was captivating, calming, and soothing to watch. Therapy for the soul. Dusk was one of the few times when the mind could safely wander through the collected images of the day; a time when the mind was allowed to stray as far as allowable from attentiveness to danger.

I was totally immersed in my thoughts when a car with two people drove over the levee and headed toward the parking area down shore from me. It looked like a couple—perhaps drawn to the river to relax, take in the vista, melt away the demands of society, or perhaps just to have sex and here I was, ruining the evening. They didn't stay long and I had to chuckle, never having pictured myself as a form of birth control.

I raccoon-proofed the gear and kayak and crawled into the tent. It was dark and time to bring the day to its end. I laid on top of the sleeping bag, revisiting in my mind the images of the day—scenes that I couldn't dwell on in depth as they went by during the course of the day. On evenings like this I could sort through, study, and refile the images. I fell asleep with visions of a breakfast plate heaped high with everything but oatmeal.

I woke early. Stepping out of the tent and looking east there was a faint hint of light in the predawn sky. Knowing breakfast would take at least an hour I packed up and got everything ready to paddle upon my return from town. After packing away the sleeping bag, matt, and tent, I brushed my teeth, wetted and combed my hair and, except for the four days growth of beard, the wrinkled tee shirt and shorts, and mud-color tennies, I would look like anyone else in the cafe.

I headed for the road going over the levee and saw the town less than a quarter mile away. I began thinking this was going to be a great way to start the day. Engaging in good conversation about my journey with people in the cafe would probably dominate the little morning oasis. I could picture it: drinking fresh strong hot coffee, eating a legendary country breakfast, and maybe even someone saying, 'Hey, let me pay for that breakfast for you.' Could it happen?

I followed the old man's directions and, after going the two blocks from the edge of town took a right onto the street and there it stood: The Satisfied Frog Cafe. An oasis from oatmeal.

The lights from inside the cafe cast a warm inviting yellow glow on the outside sidewalk in the early morning light. This could have been a scene from a Norman Rockwell painting. With each step, the laughter and conversational bantering got louder. The closer I got, the more energized and excited I became. I looked in the window as I passed the cafe front and noticed a group of about 15 people, all men, sitting at a half dozen or so different tables. Their laughter was infectious and I was already smiling as I opened the screen door to the cafe.

I stepped in with a big smile and stopped to look around, wanting to locate a seat at a table. When the screen door closed behind me, all eyes in the cafe looked my way, smiles dropped, talk stopped, and the place went dead silent. I stood there, wondering 'what the hell happened?' A half second ago the place was raucous with conversation; you could hear the proverbial pin drop right now.

I inconspicuously checked my pants fly—safe there. What could it be? My smile left me and I imagine I had a cornered dog look when I finally realized I was the victim of the "stranger among us" situation. Even the waitress came out from the hidden kitchen area to see what had happened.

There was no one sitting at the counter so I quickly eliminated my original thought of sitting amongst the other cafe dwellers. I could smell food and short of anything but a death threat, I wasn't leaving until I had a large plate of it. With a confident walk I headed for the counter while nearly every eye in the place followed me. When I got there, the waitress said she would be with me right away and disappeared into the kitchen. Sitting there I glanced quickly over my shoulder. No one was saying a word. I took the menu from its holder by the sugar jar in front of me and the humor of the situation began to bring a half smile to my face. Maybe it was the smile, or the length of the awkward moment that caused a couple of fellows at a nearby table to begin talking, although the conversation was low in tone and quiet.

After delivering a couple orders, passing out some friendly 'good mornings,' the waitress finally approached with a hint of a smile and pulled out the order pad from her apron.

"Now what can I get for you," she asked? I ordered the special—two eggs, two sausages, hash browns, toast, coffee, plus a side order of biscuits and gravy, with a request to start with the coffee right away.

A few other conversations had started back up, but the cafe was still only a small murmur compared to its vibrant sounds just moments before I had entered. I wondered if my presence would ever allow them to carry on the unguarded conversation that existed before my appearance.

I spent the next 15 minutes studying the cafe items on the wall in front of me and analyzing the situation. I knew these guys all knew each other and probably knew most everything there was to know about each other. And they knew each other knew! They were comfortable with their place in the group and had probably been coming to the cafe for years, sitting at the same tables, and probably in the same chairs. It was a club of sorts, and familiarity was the passport to membership— something I definitely did not have.

The exciting morning breakfast picture I had envisioned at

camp this morning was falling apart very quickly. It was obvious there was not going to be any engaging conversation. At least none in which I was going to be allowed to participate. There was not going to be any telling of the journey and there sure as hell wasn't going to be anyone saying, 'Here, let me buy that breakfast for you.' Not that any of those things really mattered. At this point, I just hoped the food was going to be good!

The two-plate breakfast was placed in front of me. It looked and smelled good, and it looked like a lot. I began eating and was only half aware of the guys behind me when I heard one ask a fellow at the next table over how much rain he got yesterday out at his place. The guy answered, "I got nearly an inch." Then he counter-questioned with, "How much at your place?" The guy behind me answered "two inches." "One in the rain gauge by the barn and an inch in the rain gauge by the garden." It was an obvious ploy to relax the group and it worked. Several men were now chuckling and there was less attention placed on the presence of the stranger at the counter.

I continued eating, thoroughly enjoying the meal but filling up fast. My stomach was not used to the volume and bulk of the food that sat in front of me. But I wasn't leaving until I ate it all. Who knows when an opportunity like this might arise again?

By the time I finished eating, the noise level was at about half of its original sound. Although I had been in the cafe over a half hour, my presence still had an effect on the farmer-type group of men sitting at the tables. Swallowing the last bit of coffee I stood up, slipped a damp five dollar bill under the three dollar meal check. As I turned to leave, all eyes were again on me and the conversation noise level dropped.

I walked out of the cafe and into the morning light. I was

full and satisfied, which got me thinking about the name of the cafe. I briefly thought of going back inside to inquire, but then canceled the thought for fear of screwing up all those conversations again.

I smiled and began walking back to the kayak, the river, and the journey. I had reached a point where I was beginning to feel more comfortable on the water than I did on the land.

When I reached the crest of the levee, I turned back and looked at the town of Keithsburg. It may have have been the safest place on earth, but it sure wasn't the friendliest.

## MAD DOG AND SKEET

Looking at the map, Cottonwood Point situated on the Arkansas, Missouri line on the west bank of the river seemed to be my best camping opportunity. While the river banks on both sides on this stretch of river were cut vertically by the current, Cottonwood Point seemed to provide good river access. I envisioned an old ferry boat landing, a fishing boat launching ramp, or at least a place to land to get off the river for the night.

I had an hour left of daylight to get off the river and make camp. Cottonwood Point was about two miles down river which translated to about 16 minutes of paddling time. The river was straight and there were no obvious changes in the bank structure as far as I could see. I paddled in closer to the west bank, not wanting to pass by the landing and face the task of having to paddle back upstream against the current to backtrack.

Up ahead on the high bank I could see the top half of an old two-story building .It was located near where the map indicated the landing should be. Just ahead there was a wide groove in the bank which turned out to be a little less steep than the bank on either side. It was filled with really large rocks with river silt filling in the spaces between them, providing a smooth surface—and a good enough spot for me to get off the river for the night.

I pulled up onto the narrow two-foot wide beach and, after pulling the kayak up onto shore, turned to look up at the bank. It was almost 50 feet to the top. Tying the craft to a two-inch thick stick I had wedged between two rocks, I climbed up, carrying the tent and sleeping pad, having already decided this is the place to camp.

At the top of the bank I found myself standing among large willows and tall weeds, with an old two-story house perched about 30 yards to my right. It looked abandoned so I decided to head over there, thinking it might offer a cleared area in which to set up the tent.

Stepping over a broken down fence, I could see that the yard area around the house had been mowed some time back. It was obvious the house had not been lived in and the driveway was not well used. Perhaps someone was occasionally mowing the grass just to keep the weeds at bay?

Deciding the odds were low that someone would be visiting this place between now and the time I left in the morning, I decided to put up the tent in the mowed area between the house and riverbank, opposite to where the driveway came in.

I climbed back down the bank to retrieve the rest of my gear and ensure the kayak was secured for the night. For the first time since the journey began, the craft would be out of my sight. The kayak was the journey and I had almost always had it in sight. This was an uneasy feeling.

Returning to my tent site I glanced back in the direction of the unattended kayak, when I saw through the weeds a car parked only 40 yards away. Two guys were sitting in it, both watching me. My first thought was to wonder where the heck they had come from and how had I missed seeing them earlier when I was walking around the house.

My next thought was to wonder what I should do. I could see the guy on the passenger side of the car. He was wearing a red bandanna head band, wasn't' smiling, and didn't look real friendly. The conversation I was having with myself centered on whether to talk to them or ignore them

In an effort to buy more analyzing time, I decided to wave— kind of a cool James Dean type wave that any guy wearing a red bandanna head band and sleeveless shirt would respond to. There was no response. I thought, 'What now, Ron?'

I needed to get some idea of the camping risk level here. If this was not a good situation, I needed to know real soon. Apparently, the only way I was going to find out was to go over and check things out first hand. I looked down and calmly kicked the gear bag closer to the tent, just to be doing something and to demonstrate that getting over to talk to them was not my top priority. Walking down alongside the house in the mowed area, I picked my way through the weeds. Getting closer, I could see the car was an early model, well-used Oldsmobile. Lying on the ground outside the passenger's window were several fresh empty beer cans.

'Great,' I thought. 'Half drunk and unfriendly.' Too late to turn around now, I raised my voice above the music coming from the car and asked, "Do you think anybody would mind if I camped over there?" motioning toward the tent. The guy on the passenger's side just sat and looked at me, not saying a word. The driver, however, reached over and turned the music down.

I was now standing about two feet from the passenger's door. Bending down, I used a different approach, telling them I didn't mean to interrupt "you good ole' boys party, but do you think anyone would mind if I camped there tonight?"

Wanting to give them some power over permission to camp, I followed with, "I'm not from around here and I don't want to get anyone mad." There was a pause and then the driver asked: "You're not from around here, are you?" I chuckled inside, thinking isn't that what I had just said. I told him he was right; that I was canoeing down the river to New Orleans. He replied "You got a long ways to go. When you supposed to be there?"

I smiled inside, again, thinking this was the first time anyone had thought of the journey as a transportation issue. The guy in the passenger side of the car took a drink of his beer and asked me where I was from in a tone of genuine curiosity. Telling him my background, I told him that I had paddled somewhere around 1,800 miles so far. Again there was a pause and a pondering glaze in his eyes and he questioned me whether that was a long ways to go. I just smiled and told him it was and that I was hot and hungry.

The driver reached into the case of beer between them on the seat and offered me one. I couldn't believe it. Five minutes ago I was wondering if these guys were a threat and now they were offering me beer. Beer seems to be the social lubricant of the river.

I enthusiastically said yes, that I would 'kill for a cold beer about now,' and then immediately wondered about my choice of words. The driver handed me the can and I noticed it was the same kind as on the ground at my feet, indicating that I had been right in thinking they had been here the whole time I was setting up camp. Told them "My name's Ron; I sure appreciate the beer." And I immediately opened the can and began drinking.

The guy in the driver's seat nodded toward his buddy and said his name was Skeet and that "They call me Mad Dog." Looking at each in turn, giving a nod, and holding up a salute with the beer can, I said: "Skeet, Mad Dog, nice to meet you guys" and I left it at that.

I finished the beer in three big drinks and it didn't go unnoticed. I crushed the can with my hands for the redneck affect and tossed it onto the new pile of cans at my feet. I definitely didn't condone littering but this didn't seem to be the time or place to start an environmental movement. "When in Rome...?"

Mad Dog instantly reached back into the beer carton, pulling out another beer suggesting I could use another one. I thanked him, telling him I had forgotten to taste the first one.

I was still thirsty but I drank the second beer a little slower as we talked about the river, local towns, cars, and what it was like up in Minnesota. Neither of them had been north. Both were in their early forties, slender, and with long hair. Skeet's was gathered and tied into something of a ponytail in back below the head band. He had a number of tattoos on his arms, one of which was a well-done black panther with red claw marks.

Mad Dog's hair was not as long as Skeet's and was a little less than shoulder length and unkempt. I was thinking to myself that these guys were pretty scruffy looking when I realized I was probably just as scruffy as they were. I must have looked like a river bum, with weather-beaten face, dry, wind-blown straw hair, and two days growth of beard. Dressed in dirty, wrinkled clothing, they were probably feeling sorry for me when they offered the refreshments.

I was on my third beer when Pete reached forward, opened the glove compartment, and pulled out a baggie with 15 to 20 little white pills in it. He reached in the bag and took one out, popping it into his mouth and washing it down with beer. He handed the bag to Mad Dog who repeated the ceremony. Mad Dog then closed the bag and set it on the seat, just as I am thinking that I'm off the hook on the white pills. But then Mad Dog picks up the bag, hands it my way, and says, "Here's what you need; take two."

When I asked what it was, Mad Dog replied, "Those are little white crosses." When I asked what they did for a person, Skeet, now holding out two pills, informs me, "You take those and you will be in New Orleans by tomorrow night."

This was the last type of situation I wanted to be in, but both men were now looking at me, watching my response while Skeet continued to hold out his hand with the two pills. I stuck out my cupped hand and took them, enthusiastically saying, "Thanks, I won't be on the river again until morning, but I can sure use them then." Holding the pills in one hand I immediately took a long drink of beer to gain some thinking time. When I finished, I told them I was going to be cooking some rice for dinner and asked if they wanted to join me, hoping the dinner offer would show I was trying to repay them for their gift of dope; secondly, to direct attention away from the fact that I hadn't taken the pills. My third motive was to create a way to quickly and legitimately part company by implying I was leaving soon to cook dinner.

Skeet, now looking forward, just shook his head. Mad Dog looked at me with an expression I couldn't read and said, "No thanks, not hungry."

I took a couple more drinks from the beer to finish it, faked a tired stretch, and said I had better get dinner cooking. I leaned down, looking at both Mad Dog and Skeet through the open window and said, "If you boys change your minds about food, it'll be right over there," motioning toward the tent. I re-thanked them for the beer, gave a wave, and walked back to the tent.

About 20 minutes had passed since I first set up the tent, but there was still enough light to cook without a flashlight. While fixing the chicken and rice meal, I analyzed the encounter, feeling it had been amicable enough. But, on the other hand, these boys were both getting pretty messed up on alcohol and pills. My overall gut feeling, however, was that everything was okay.

It was dark now, and I was putting away gear for the night when I heard them start the car and let it run for awhile before turning on the lights. I listened to the noise of the car fade as it distanced itself from me on the gravel road nearby. It seemed I could hear that car for a long time, That was good; if they came back I would be able to hear them long before they reached the tent.

I crawled into the tent and stretched out on the bag. I hoped the evening with Mad Dog and Skeet was over. But I found myself reflecting again on the generosity of people on and along the river, and how it stretches across all social classes. I had been offered everything from wine from folks on a yacht, to dope from guys in an Oldsmobile. What was the impetus for such offers to a stranger on the river? Such generosity did not seem to happen to strangers going through a strange town.

The night was breezy in the open area where I was camped. I was aware of the tents nylon covering wavering in the breeze on and off all night. That's why I was surprised by the vehicle that pulled up next to the house at the crack of dawn. I thought I would have heard it coming before it got to me. I lay there awake, clearing the sleep from my mind when I heard the vehicle door open and shut and the footsteps of someone approaching the tent. I threw off the cover of the sleeping bag, unzipped the door of the tent, and stepped out, wanting to face whoever was coming.

The man just passed the tent as I scrambled out. He looked back, grinning, and said, "Sorry to wake you; I'm checking the river gauge," and he motioned to a vertical culvert sticking out of the ground 20 yards away. I had seen it the evening before but hadn't paid much attention to it. I gave a nod and crawled back into the tent, wondering who the heck checks river gauges this early in the day? At least it explained the mowed grass.

Before long, water was heating for the oatmeal and coffee. I picked up the coffee cup that I had placed the two pills in last night, just in case Mad Dog and Skeet had shown up for dinner and wanted them back if I wasn't going to use them that night.

I gave them a disgusted fling over the bank into the weeds. I needed coffee!

I broke camp and loaded up the kayak—which was safe and sound despite my worries. I pushed off and began paddling, realizing I was still tired but comforted by the fact I was on the river again. Thinking back on all that had happened last night, I found myself in silent prayer that tonight's camp would be an island or sand bar.

One of the very few pictures taken of me on the lower Mississippi. I was told I didn't make a very big picture out on the water.

## DUANE AND MARSO DEBOISE

The river had narrowed to less than a mile wide just above Morganza, Louisiana. I was making good time at five to six miles per hour, and feeling rather good for having put 61 miles behind me this day. I had less than two hours of paddling left before making camp for the night.

I had my eye on a Jon boat that had, what looked like two guys in it, making its way up the river on the opposite bank. When I was directly across from them, I noticed that the "other guy" was in fact a big dog sitting on the bow seat and looking up river.

I instinctively gave a wave with the paddle, not knowing if the person in the boat running the motor was looking at me. After all, as others along the river had pointed out, I didn't make a very big picture on the river. I wasn't real surprised, however, when he raised his arm and waved back. I had come to know that most people who spend time on these waters were very alert to their surroundings, fully aware of the consequences of not being attentive.

It was after 7 P.M. and I had begun looking for a suitable place to camp. About a mile down the river on the west bank was a light-colored area, suggesting it might be a sandy place to land. Good camping spots were getting harder to find on the lower end of the Mississippi. Good level spots were more often than not, covered with soft, Mississippi mud rather than nice dry sand.

Mississippi mud is the greasiest, stickiest, "stain-ingest" stuff you can get on yourself or your clothes. It's nearly impossible to get it out of your shoes or clothes or even off the kayak. I found out the hard way never to step in it with your shoes on if you ever want to see them again. I began to learn to go barefoot—you always got your feet back and they were easier to clean than shoes.

The light-colored area was not sand, but turned out to be the ever-present concrete revetment placed along the bank to control erosion. It wasn't as good as sand for banking the kayak, but it certainly beat Mississippi mud. After finding a spot on the 10-foot high bank on which to pitch my tent, I returned to the shore to get my gear. When I reached the kayak I heard an outboard motor and spotted the guy and his dog in the Jon boat that I had seen two hours earlier up river. They were coming down river on my side and the man had stopped, his motions indicating that he was checking fish traps or fish lines alongside of the boat.

Watching only for a moment, I grabbed my gear, headed up the bank and finished pitching the tent when he and his dog motored up to within a 100 yards of where I was camped. The dog jumped out of the boat and began barking in my direction, then disappeared into the woods. The man reached over his boat, picked up a set line and began checking it for fish.

I continued my evening supper ritual, glancing periodically at his work; he occasionally glanced my way checking my interest in what he was doing. I had just sat down to eat my supper when he finished his work and, without saying a word, revved up the motor and headed towards shore. Just as the bow touched the shoreline the dog reappeared from the woods, ran straight for the boat, and jumped into the bow seat. The guy backed away from shore and headed my way. As he approached I donned a friendly smile and nodded, knowing he couldn't hear anything I might try to say above the noise of the motor. When he was directly in front of me he cut the power of the motor and shouted "Can I get you anything?

The question caught me off guard. It wasn't the usual opening conversation, questioning where I was coming from or where I was headed. Seeing me earlier nearly 10 miles up river, he must have figured out I was traveling.

I was low on drinking water and told him I could use some water or anything to drink. He powered up the motor and headed toward me. I set my food on a level chunk of concrete and scrambled down the bank to catch the bow of the boat, hoping the black labrador retriever was friendly. He commanded the dog to stay and, after sniffing me briefly, the dog turned his attention to his master.

"Well trained dog," I commented.

"Name's Marso De Boise," the boat captain answered.

"Glad to meet you, I'm Ron."

He stopped rummaging, looked back at me and, with a partial grin said, "That's the dog's name, not mine."

Caught off guard I just muttered "oh" and countered that it was an interesting name for a dog and wondering how he got such a name. The captain just answered that he thought it would be a good name for that dog.

He pulled a six-pack of Sprite from a cooler compartment behind the rear seat and made his way to the front of the boat through an array of hooks, lines, and nets. It was obvious the dog made a point not to leave the bow seat to avoid stepping on a hook on the floor. Probably was a lesson well learned.

When he reached the front of the boat he held out the six pack and asked if this would do since he didn't have any water. I told him one would be fine but he insisted on my taking the entire pack, telling me he was "done for the day."

The dog barked a few times, indicating he wanted to leave the boat and join us on the bank. The man gave an arm signal toward the woods and the dog immediately jumped from the boat, stopping briefly to sniff me and then again, headed for the woods. I was hoping he wasn't headed for the supper I had left sitting on the rock.

"Care to come sit a spell while I finish eating?" I asked him, turning and heading up the bank and sensing the need to get there before the dog did. We found suitable rocks, five feet apart, to sit on and enjoy a good view of the evening sky as dusk approached. He started the conversation by asking me what I was eating. I told him it was sour cream, chives, and noodles and offered him some. He shook his head and, with a pause, asked me if it was any good. I told him I'd had better but it kept me alive. That half grin came over his face again.

The conversation was slow at first, unlike most I had had on the river. Usually they started with the "who," "what," "when," and "where" questions in rapid fire. This conversation, on the other hand, was relaxing. I would ask a question; he would answer. There would be a pause and then he would ask a question and I would answer, followed by another pause. I could tell he was interested in "The Story" but he obviously didn't want to pry. I focused on information about this stretch of the river, this part of Louisiana, or the fishing business—keeping things general. I had learned that people on the river are extremely generous and friendly, but very private. Almost no personal questions were ever asked and almost never did I learn people's last names. After he had answered a question it was as if he had earned the right to ask another, but he would never ask several questions in a row. It made for unique conversation.

We talked until the last remnants of light began to fade in the clear evening sky and then he stood up, saying he didn't have any lights on the boat and that he should be heading for the landing a half mile down river. As we stepped down the bank, he said he would be back on the river early in the morning and could drop off anything I might need from a store.

Since I was usually packed and paddling shortly after daybreak, I told him thanks, but that I would probably be gone by the time he came by.

"I doubt that," he said. "I will be here at daybreak."

If that were the case, I listed a gallon of water and, if he brought a thermos of coffee I would help him drink it. "You've got it," he answered, taking the six empty Sprite bottles I had drank entirely by myself in the hour's time we had spent chatting. He no sooner started the motor and Marso De Boise came running down the bank and jumped onto the bow seat. Pushing the boat off from shore I realized I hadn't even learned my visitor's name and shouted the question across the water.

"Duane" he shouted back, and headed the boat out and down the river.

I watched him disappear into the river night, wondering if he really would show up in the morning. It didn't really matter; I had enjoyed the evening company. The mosquitoes were now having a dinner of their own and, since I was the only course, I quickly slipped into the tent. Tired as I was, I lay awake for quite awhile, thinking about the evening spent with Duane, and the endless generosity of the river people. I fell asleep, looking forward to the morning and the potential for a good cup of fresh-brewed hot coffee and more conversation.

The alarm on my watch was set for 5:50 A.M. but I almost always instinctively woke up 10 minutes before it told me to. This morning, probably in anticipation of Duane, I was awake even earlier than usual. It was still dark and so I was in no hurry to fumble around and make my breakfast.

It wasn't long when I heard the drone of an outboard motor coming up river. I was almost certain it was Duane; it was too coincidental not to be. It was a clear, cool morning and in sharp contrast to what I knew midday would bring. It would be a few minutes before Duane arrived so I got out the stove and began heating the breakfast water. For some reason I wanted the appearance that I had been up for some time. A response to some Midwestern cultural work ethic I had been raised with, I am sure.

I flicked on the mini mag flashlight to show him my location. There was barely enough light to see across the river and I thought it might be difficult for him to pick out my small camping spot against the dark background of trees behind me.

I made my way down to the same spot the boat had been pulled up to last night and again grabbed the boat as it touched the shore, lifting and pulling at the same time to land it on the concrete revetment. Marso DeBois was there to check me out, tail wagging. "Mornin," I said, "Glad to see you."

"Yea," Duane answered. "I'm running a little late this morning." I grinned, thinking he must also have the same work ethic complex.

"I brought you some water," he said, handing me a bag. "There's coffee in there for yuh."

We climbed to the top of the bank and reclaimed our spots on the same rocks from the night before. Marso DeBois was long gone, off hunting in the woods by the time we sat down. I opened the bag and took out the gallon of water, then pulled out the thermos of coffee, noting there were still other items in the bag. I hesitated, not sure if the other items were for me or him. He must have sensed my dilemma and quickly commented: "I didn't know how you took your coffee so I brought some extra stuff."

The extra "stuff" turned out to be a small container of sugar, half pint of milk, and a bag of cookies. After placing the items between us, I said: "I use 'em all in my coffee." I poured a cup for myself and handed another cup to him without asking if he wanted some. With a touch of a smile on his face, he took it. Although I seldom put anything in my coffee, I added both milk and sugar, appreciating the added calories for the workday ahead.

The freshly brewed coffee was delicious compared to the instant coffee I was used to making on cool or rainy mornings. I expressed my delight and then took two cookies from the bag, placing it near him without asking if he wanted any. A few minutes later, he helped himself and then we easily picked up the conversation where we had left off the evening before.

He wanted to know "The Story" in as much detail as time would permit. As we talked and drank coffee, I fixed my instant oatmeal breakfast and ate in between sips of coffee and bites of cookies. He attentively watched my breakfast process and then asked me if I have oatmeal every morning. I told him, 'every morning.' A few moments later he said, "You can take those cookies with you." I began to chuckle, suggesting that he thought my oatmeal breakfast looked "that bad." Duane agreed and said "Yep!"

It was getting light out and we had finished breakfast. We both had things that needed to be done today and each knew this chance encounter would come to an end sooner or later. Duane stood up, indicating it was time to part ways. He said he had lines to check and that he had "better be gettin' to it." I agreed, saying I had miles to paddle. I picked up the thermos, leftover milk and sugar and, keeping the cookies separate, handed the bag back to him, thanking him. He didn't say a word and we walked down to the boat without talking, standing for a moment and looking out over the fast moving river.

We knew the odds were great that we would never meet again. As he got into the boat, I said: "Have a good life, Duane." As the motor started, he replied, "You, too." No sooner had the engine sounded when Marso DeBoise came running and claimed his rightful place in the bow seat. Duane backed the boat out into the river, turned the bow upstream, shifted from reverse to forward and began moving up river. We both gave one final wave goodbye. I stood on the bank and watched for a short while as he cut across the river to the other side.

Like any other morning, I quickly cleaned up and stowed the gear in the kayak. On this journey, if I wasn't paddling, I wasn't going anywhere. Before climbing into the kayak, I took one last look up river to see if I could see Duane. I couldn't. As the paddle struck the water, I wondered if our paths would ever cross again and if this encounter, or any of the others on

# The
# Third
# Danger

100+ degree temperatures with humidity in the 70 percent range seemed to be the norm on the lower reaches of the river. Physical problems caused by heat were a daily concern.

## RIVER CURRENT

The river current was dangerous—like carrying a snake in your pocket. You never really knew if it would strike and, if it did, just when. Your undivided attention was the only defense you had and you were constantly aware of your relationship to the river.

River current is the first and always imminent danger of the river and it demonstrated its need for daily attention. The most dramatic example of its potential to strike unexpectedly was at a stretch of river named "Sunflower Bend" just above Rosedale, Mississippi. The strong current had laid the huge river buoys over, pointing them downstream at a steep angle. The buoys looked as if they were dancing as they bobbed up and down and slipped back and forth, trying to right themselves against the current.

Looking down river from the kayak, it appeared like there was a perceptible drop in the river. Several times I had seen current boils like these take one of those large buoys under, only to see it immediately free itself from the current and pop back up. However, in one instance, I watched it take one down a hundred yards ahead of me and I never saw it pop back up to the surface. I knew it would—sooner or later, but when? I had seen the buoy's location so I knew I could stay clear of the area should it decide to pop back up as I paddled over it.

The question in my mind now was how many up ahead were just like this one, waiting to pop back up at any moment? And where were they? The river had my full attention again. There were no barges in sight so I moved outward to the middle of the channel to take advantage of the swift current and paddle where it hopefully would be safe from unexpected buoys popping up underneath. I paddled on high alert for several miles before I was confident the current had slowed enough so as not to contain any surprise jack-in-the-box buoys.

The prop washes from the barge tows created huge waves and a wild turbulence in the river's current.

## BOATS

The second gravest danger was boat traffic. Above Minneapolis, it was the high speed recreational traffic and, more often than not, under the influence of alcohol. Below Minneapolis, it was the barge traffic. Operation of barges themselves did not cause undue alarm as they were big and slow. It was what they did to the current around them that caused the danger.

The prop washes were powerful and cause a wild turbulence in the current. A river traveler had to always be vigilant so as not to get caught on the cut bank side of the river behind a barge going up river. The props' wash could easily jam you into the revetment on the bank, causing you to flip and be pulled down by an undertow or swept down river along the broken rock or concrete and steel revetment. The life jacket was always on in the vicinity of barges.

Below Baton Rouge it was the combination of barge traffic and ocean-going ship traffic that held my attention. The shipping traffic was almost constant from Baton Rogue through New Orleans to the Gulf. The ocean-going ships produced huge waves that would begin to break as they hit the shallower waters outside the shipping channel. I made an extra effort to keep the kayak in deep water when the ships passed. This allowed me to ride up over the rolling, 5 to 6-foot swells, instead of trying to paddle through breakers crashing over the deck of the kayak in shallower water. Boats always presented a valid danger, albeit an intermittent one.

## WEATHER

The third danger, like the first two, was a daily one. Weather. It was subtle, most times not as threatening as currents or boat traffic. My first lesson came eight days into the journey. I was paddling a stretch of the river above Brainerd, Minnesota. It was mid-afternoon and I could see a group of islands up ahead that broke the river into several channels. I had just looked at the river map a third time in the last minute, trying to determine the route of the river channel. I would look at the map, determine where the channel was, put the map down, pick up the paddle, start to paddle and then soon question myself about which side of the island the channel was on.

After the third time, I was cursing myself and wondering 'what the problem was with Ron' and why couldn't he figure it out? 'Make a decision,' I said to myself. I knew there was a problem but I passed it off as just being tired of paddling. I was always tired of paddling by mid-afternoon. I eventually got passed the islands but continued to have a nagging notion that what I had just experienced should not be happening.

Luckily, I was scheduled to meet my wife Lila that evening at Brainerd for equipment exchanges. The first eight days of travel were to have been the shake-down period for determining what equipment and supplies I would need for the rest of the journey. We had gotten a motel room near the river to spend the night.

Did that soft bed feel good! The bathroom hosted a weight scale and, despite my earlier anticipation that I might lose a little weight, I found I had dropped 11 pounds on the first eight days of the journey. I told Lila that, at this rate I would return as half the man I started as. We tried to analyze whether I needed to carry bigger meals.

Lila asked how much water I was going through each day. After thinking about it, I realized that the current two-liter bottle of water had sat for two days. I was drinking less than a liter of water per day. The weather had been cloudy, cool and often drizzly and I wasn't working up a sweat, thus there was seldom the desire for a drink. It became obvious that I was becoming dehydrated. The weight loss, fatigue, and poor ability to analyze and make decisions were symptoms of dehydration.

After a huge breakfast and a new policy for water intake, I continued the journey the next morning. I would drink water every hour, on the hour, for each hour I was on the river—no matter the weather. It became a personal law that I would consume a minimum of two liters of water daily. I was carrying six liters which meant I had at least three days worth when fully stocked. So far I had always had access to potable water within that time span.

### Green Clouds . . . sometimes not so subtle

The rain coat and rain hat were in "reachable" distance, just beyond the life jacket on the front deck. Rain gear was held in place by the elastic cords that crisscrossed the cargo deck immediately in front of the sitting area of the kayak. Rain was an off-and-on thing during the journey and I never knew from one hour to the next if I was going to need that gear. It was too hot to wear unless I was certain of rain and, I wasn't too concerned about getting wet. The effort of paddling kept me damp or wet anyway; during a downpour I would slip the raincoat on over the spray skirt to keep the rain from getting inside the kayak and getting everything else wet.

I was on the pool just above Lock and Dam #8, north of the Minnesota/Iowa line and it was warm and overcast, looking like rain with widely scattered dark clouds crossing over the river, spitting a few drops of moisture as they passed. I heard thunder to the southwest and was hoping the storm would cross the river heading east before I got to that point.

The pool was nearly three miles wide. I was paddling in the river channel which ran close to the west bank. Bluffs that towered several hundred feet high on the west side were spectacular to behold but blocked my view of the western sky; I could only guess where the rumbling of thunder was coming from, and how far away. Analyzing the potential of being caught in a thunderstorm, I figured the high bluffs would offer some protection from strong winds or lightning, as long as the storm came more from the west than south. Like most of the rainstorms I had encountered thus far, I figured I could throw on the raincoat and ride it out while paddling down river.

Only minutes later it became obvious I was going to be in the path of that storm. Dark clouds were rising into view from behind the bluffs. I began paddling closer to shore, thinking this one could be an angry one. By now I was searching for shelter. The highway was carved out between the bluff and the river and a steep rock bank dropped from the highway guard rail right to river's edge.

The bank allowed few trees to grow that might provide shelter and not any large enough to lean out over the river. I wasn't sure I wanted to be under a tree anyway. There weren't any bridges that I could see that might cross a creek coming from one of several bluff valleys. There were some large culverts coming out from under the highway but 'Mama Severs didn't raise no fool,' I thought. I wasn't about to take shelter in a culvert in a thunderstorm.

It was starting to rain hard and I was resigned to toughing it out on the water until I looked up. The clouds were no longer dark grey, but an ominous swirling green. "Oh shit, this is not good," I said out loud. From my experience, nothing good ever came from swirling green clouds. I started thinking that Mama Severs did, perhaps, raise a fool. Passing a small point caused by a protrusion of the bluff into the river, I spotted a small cove formed on the down river side of the point. In the cove were some larger-sized trees growing on the steep bank close to the shoreline. I figured they were going to be my best bet for finding shelter.

At this point, I forgot about lightning. Trees on the bluff above me would more likely be a target than these trees down along the river. Paddling as fast as I could, I reached a large box elder hanging out over the river and got under it as far as possible. At best, the tree's crown covered about half of the kayak. I made sure to get into that half, put the paddle down on the rocky shore, grabbed hold of a rock to keep the kayak steady with one hand, and was closing up the rain coat tightly with the other hand when all hell broke loose.

An ever-increasing roar changed to a crashing noise. I instinctively folded into a tight-sitting, fetal position with no idea what to expect. Within a split second I saw the first large hail stone hit the water in front of me, followed by thousands more. I let out a sigh of relief, thinking that is all this was. I had imagined a tornado or a car from the highway above, or a tree crashing down upon me. The old box elder was shedding most of the hail, but tattered and broken green leaves were falling like the hail that was shredding them. Most of that hail was the size of quarters.

I was beginning to wonder if there were enough leaves on that tree to outlast the storm and protect me from the hail. Trees may or may not have sensory perception, but I was sure thanking this one for being there and taking such a beating for me. I sat there, recalling an account I had read of Lewis and Clark's men being caught in a severe hail storm at the Great Falls portage. The hail was so large it nearly killed them and they returned to camp, battered and bruised. I began thinking out a plan for the next time this might happen and if I weren't fortunate enough to find a box elder! That plan pictured me with the padded life jacket over my head and shoulders and sliding as far down into the kayak as possible.

The hail storm passed and the rain began to let up. Picking up the paddle, I pushed away from shore and out from under that tree. It was totally shredded, looking like it had been blasted by a gigantic shotgun. I again thanked the tree for its' shelter and, with the kayak plastered with wet pieces of leaves, I resembled a giant green bean heading down river.

Watching the storm moving east, I realized it had been a close one.

## HEAT

It was 103 degrees the day I reached Greenville, Mississippi. Pulling the kayak up over the top of the rocky, 30-foot bank, in the dark, I collapsed on the mowed grass—hot and exhausted.

The map had shown the location of the campground along the river. I had planned to reach it by evening. Any mistakes I made now were costly. My northern body found every day to be a hot one on the river as it passed through these southern states. High humidity, reflecting sun off the water, and no shade made for long hot days. I wore a baseball cap bill for a visor to reduce the reflection off the water. Much of the time I paddled with a wet T-shirt draped over my head for a cooling effect.

The day seemed no different than the previous day until mid-afternoon. I was hitting the mid-afternoon physiological lows—something I had come to expect on the journey and for which I had to mentally prepare myself. This was different. I was tired, really tired. I leaned forward and rested my head on my arm on the deck in front of me. The brief rest felt good and allowed me time to collect my thoughts. I automatically began a self-check on my mental and physical condition.

Whether it was my hot dry skin or the lack of color in the scenery around me that first drew my attention, but the two symptoms were telling me something was not right. My upper arm, normally warm, actually felt hot and dry to the touch. It was a symptom I knew was related to heat exhaustion.

The lack of color puzzled me. I was thinking it might be

caused by the reflecting sunlight off the water and maybe a symptom related to something like snow blindness. In any case, I felt a strong need to get off the river and deal with the situation. Taking several big drinks of the warm water from the bottle, I began a non-strenuous but deliberate paddle toward shore.

I found a spot on the revetment where I could practically land the kayak and hold it against the current long enough for me to climb out. Once out, I pulled the craft up onto the revetment and tied it to one of the iron rebars. I took another big drink then dug out a granola bar from the food bag. With no shade on the river side of the levy system, I was forced to find a comfortable sitting spot in the sun and put the wet T-shirt back over my head. The idea then occurred to me that it made some sense to submerse myself into the river water. Many evenings, if the camping location wasn't too muddy, I would take a quick bath in the river to remove the sweat and grime of the day and cool down before going to sleep. A wet body in an evening breeze always has a cool effect; it should work here.

I looked for a spot to slip into the river. The current was strong and I would need to find a spot where I could hold onto something to prevent being carried down river. I found where a piece of iron rebar was sticking about two feet out of the river. Holding on, I gently lowered myself in. The water had a cooling, almost chilling effect and I was surprised at how cold the warm river water felt on my head . . . so good! I would lift my head, take a deep breath and then lower back into the water, holding my head under water for as long as I could.

I continued this routine for nearly a half hour, stretched out in the current like superman flying and periodically kicking my legs to keep some unseen aquatic critters at bay who kept biting at my legs.

When I climbed out of the river, the scenery color was back to normal and I felt cool and refreshed. I began to wonder how the loss of a hour of paddling, an equivalent of four to five miles of distance, might prevent me from making the Greenville Campground by dark. Darkness came at 7:30 and it was now 4 P.M. I still had 20 miles of paddling to reach the campground.

It felt almost good to be back on the river, making miles after that refreshing 40-minute break. I had been averaging 60 to 70 miles of river a day since leaving Cairo, Illinois where the Ohio River joins the Mississippi. I felt I could make the campground by dark but decided not to push it after what had just happened. I also decided that drinking water had to be taken every half-hour. It was harder to come by on the lower river than on the upper because most all development was a considerable distance behind the levies and there wasn't much recreation on the lower river. But liquid was needed.

The day's paddle was over. Hot and tired, once again, it felt incredibly good to be sitting on the grass, considering how dangerous the heat had been. After a bit I headed up to the registration trailer to get permission to camp. A smiling, older lady answered the door and said it would be fine to camp where I indicated I was. Then she inquisitively asked, "Have you been out on that river all day?" When I nodded, she told me in a concerned voice that it had been 103 degrees today and that I was lucky I "hadn't been cooked." She retrieved a six-pack of Coke from the back of the trailer, offered me one, and then introduced herself as Kay Roberson. I finished my soda in four quick gulps and she leaned out and handed the other four cans to me saying: "I'll bet you can drink all of these." We talked for a while and she mentioned tomorrow's temperatures were to rise into the 100's again. I planned to approach the journey with a little less exertion and a lot more water.

At this point in my journey, I had become more comfortable with asking people for things. I asked Kay if it would be possible to use the shower building I had passed on the way up. She got a key for me, pointed out the key return box at the edge of the patio, and instructed me to return it when I was done. After a few more minutes of chatting, I picked up my three remaining Cokes and said goodbye.

I finished off another Coke by the time I had retrieved my shampoo kit from the pack and got to the shower. It was a little after 8 P.M. and I had the place to myself. I took an extremely long, cool shower while I shaved and shampooed off the six days of river since my last good scrubbing. I returned the key and returned to camp to cook supper. Sitting at the picnic table eating the pasta noodle dinner, I drank the last Coke, thinking how close I may have come to a major over-heating problem on the river today. I vowed to stay more alert to my physiological condition and not let myself get that vulnerable again. I was restocked with drinking water; six two-liter bottles should last for two and a half days, drinking every half hour. I dozed off, laying on top of the sleeping bag and wondering how long I would be able to sleep after my major "re-hydration" effort.

## The Storm

For several days I had been dodging the small scattered afternoon thunderstorms that occurred daily along the Louisiana and Mississippi stretch of the river. This was flat country, unlike the high scenic river bluffs found further north in Tennessee, Illinois, Wisconsin, and Minnesota.

Along this stretch of river you could see the thunderstorms in the distance, and it was possible to estimate when they would get to the river. I would slow down to let one pass in front, or speed up to get beyond its point of river crossing. By this method, I had been successful in missing the brunt of the daily afternoon downpours.

I was about 25 miles up river from Baton Rouge and could see a large storm coming from the southwest. At first I thought that since the river was heading mostly southeast, there might be a possibility of getting below it and allowing it to pass north of me. However, it was 6:30 p.m .and I usually like to have camp set by 7. Analyzing the options, I elected to look for a place to camp right away and avoid being caught in the dark and in the rain.

Both sides of the river had been lined with barges for some time now, either full or empty and waiting to be picked up for transport up or down the river. Finding a suitable place to gain access to the levee was turning into a time-consuming problem with a fast-approaching storm. There was a large opening about a quarter mile ahead on the east side of the river. I headed toward it. Even if the bank were remotely suitable for camping, it would have to be the place to make camp for this night.

Clearing the last tied-off barge, I quickly paddled to shore to get a better look. About 50 yards down the revetment bank there was a possible landing site, an area that hadn't been torn up by current or barges. The top of the levy was only about 30 feet up the steep concrete revetment and there were medium-sized trees near the top where I could tie off the kayak for the night. Swinging the bow of the craft up into the current, I paddled parallel to the shore, climbed out and pulled it onto the levy.

The storm was rapidly approaching so I had to move quickly if I wanted to sleep dry this night!

I pulled the loaded kayak up to the trees and quickly tied the end of the bow rope to a tree. Unlatching the two straps securing the rear cargo hatch, I pulled out the tent, sleeping bag and pad, and the food pack. I would come back for the stove and cooking utensils after I set up the tent. Replacing the cargo hatch and reattaching one of the straps over it in case the wind came up, I picked up the gear and carried it the few yards to the top of the levy. There was high spot on a grassy opening that I quickly claimed as the tent location. Setting up camp was instinctive by now and it didn't require much thought (or time!) to complete the task.

I finished my task just as the storm hit the other side of the river. It looked and sounded nasty, packed with lightning, thunder, and wind. I was imagining the hail storm on Pool #8 all over again which elicited a controlled panic in me. I quickly threw the gear and food pack into the tent and closed it up. Hunched into the battering wind, I made my way back to the top of the levy and was shocked to see the kayak, with bow rope stretched out, the craft flopping back and forth in the wind on the concrete levee like a fishing lure on a string.

I hurried down the levee and grabbed the rope to try and stabilize it. On the one hand, I cursed myself for not thinking to tie the bow close to the tree instead of just tying off the end of the 15-foot rope to the tree. But on the other hand, I was pleased that I had at least thought enough ahead to tie the boat up. Working my way down the rope, I grabbed the bow and tried pulling it close to the tree. I was amazed at how the force of wind was causing the kayak to bounce wildly around. Just as I had the kayak close to the tree, the wind began banging it into a rock, knocking the rear cargo hatch cover loose from the one strap holding it. It was a curse/praise situation again as I admonished myself for not attaching both straps, but pleased that I had at least thought of attaching one of them.

If I lost the boat, this journey was over. However, the kayak was tied and the probability was high that the rope would hold. Without the hatch cover the journey could also very well be over. It would be hard to keep water out without it. I needed that hatch cover! I dropped the kayak while at the same time searching the revetment for the nearest big rock. Spotting a 20-30 pound chunk of concrete just a step away, I snatched up the rock and tossed it onto the spray skirt that then collapsed onto the seat.

The weight of the concrete caused the kayak to stabilize against the wind. In the same motion I turned and began running after the hatch cover that was sliding and bounding in sequence down the revetment. It was already 20 yards away and I had to jump over broken slabs of concrete that were awkwardly held together by twisted iron rerod bars, while trying to keep my eye on the hatch cover.

The cover finally lodged against a large piece of concrete with the wind flopping it up and down, ready to dislodge it any moment. I quickened my pace, concentrating now more on the placement of my feet than on the cover itself. Unable to stop my momentum on the wet concrete, I slid into the cover, banging my shin on the chunk of concrete holding it in place. I screamed "YES" as relief filled me. I looked at my leg where it had connected with the concrete; it was gouged and would be bruised for days but no major damage was done. I just then realized I was in a torrential downpour with gale force winds howling around me. In my effort to capture the hatch cover, I had not noticed it had started raining. Lowering my head against the wind and wet, I made my way back to the kayak which was now rocking in the buffeting gale but not bouncing around like earlier. Tossing in the rock had been a good idea.

In the pounding rain I carefully secured the hatch cover, using both straps this time. I again grabbed the bow handle and pulled the craft up closer to the tree, shortened the rope and retied it to the six-inch diameter trunk. The tree was bent and taking a good slapping from the wind and rain, but it seemed to be holding its own against the storm. Having had such good luck with the one piece of concrete in the kayak, I decided a couple more pieces would be appropriate for good measure.

My adrenaline pump had been working a long time and I began to feel physically drained. The rain actually began to hurt as it stung the exposed portions of my arms and legs. I began making my way back up the levee to the tent, with a back glance to see that the kayak wasn't moving at all.

My problems weren't over, however, As I turned to the tent I saw that the storm had blown it down, pulling out both rope stakes and two side tent stakes. The soaked tent was driven flat to the ground except for the two lumps formed by the packs inside. I tried to re-set the stakes but the ground was so soft by now that there was nothing solid to hold them. I headed back to the levee in hopes of finding some chunks of concrete to set on top of the stakes and ropes. It took six trips to locate six big rocks to do the job—one for each of the pole rope stakes at opposite ends of the tent, and one for each corner.

The adrenaline rush was over and it was almost dark. Catching glimpses of little branchlets torn from nearby trees fly through the air, I thought of yelling out to the storm: "Is that all you have got left in you?" But I figured it was not the time to taunt fate. Surveying the situation and assuming the steel barges along the levee would be a bigger attraction for lightning than I was, I decided I had done all I could do.

I took my soaked t-shirt off, wrung it out and threw it into the tent. I did the same thing with my shorts and then scrambled inside. Using my t-shirt, I wiped the rain off me as well as

I could and, after laying the sleeping pad on the wet tent floor, pulled the dry sleeping bag from its waterproof bag, placed it on the damp sleeping pad, and stretched out on top. My damp skin felt cooling in the 80 degree night air.

The day had exhausted me and it felt good just to lay still. I thought about supper but it wouldn't happen tonight. It just wasn't worth the effort.

The wind continued to batter the tent through the night. Through the wind I heard the cracking of a tree or branch to the north of the tent and I knew it must be close. Surprisingly, I was passive about the possible danger and thought, "What the hell, Ron, you think you are going to live forever?" Lying awake isn't going to prevent anything from happening. This turned out to be one of the few mornings I didn't awaken to my watch alarm and I slept in longer than usual. Lying there, still on top of the sleeping bag, I heard birds signing and figured I must have made it through the night or else heaven sounds a lot like birds in a Louisiana morning.

The day dawned bright and sunny, with water standing almost everywhere except for the small high spot on which the tent was perched. Surveying the damage, I saw a split and broken tree branch from a larger tree just to my north; it must have been the tree breaking noise I heard during the night. The rest of the world around me looked okay.

The priority for the morning was to move everything out onto the levee to expose it to the morning sun and breeze to try and dry it out. Next I turned the kayak upside down to drain out the rainwater. Once everything was set to drying I started cooking breakfast (which included the supper I didn't' get to cook last night). I was hungry and I was determined not to leave until I had eaten both.

Sipping hot coffee immediately turned me into an entirely

different person. The taste was great and somehow the dangers and hardships experienced the evening before left in the steam of the coffee. The warm morning sun beat onto my back while I sat on the levee holding the warm cup of coffee with both hands. Looking out on the river I couldn't help but realize what a difference a day can make. I was in no hurry this morning. I ate two packets of instant raisin oatmeal and then began cooking he Lipton rice pilaf intended for the evening before.

It was nearly 9:30 by the time I finished eating and packed the now-dry gear. Untying the kayak from the revetment, I looked back for one last look. It had been quite a night but with a full stomach and renewed spirit, I anticipated a great day ahead.

Later in the day I talked to a man on a tow boat who said the winds of the evening had been clocked at 76 miles per hour and had broken the radio antenna off his tow. Thinking back, I realized how good a decision it had been to camp when I did and not risk being caught on the water when the storm hit.

Was the decision luck? Or was it becoming a journey survival instinct?

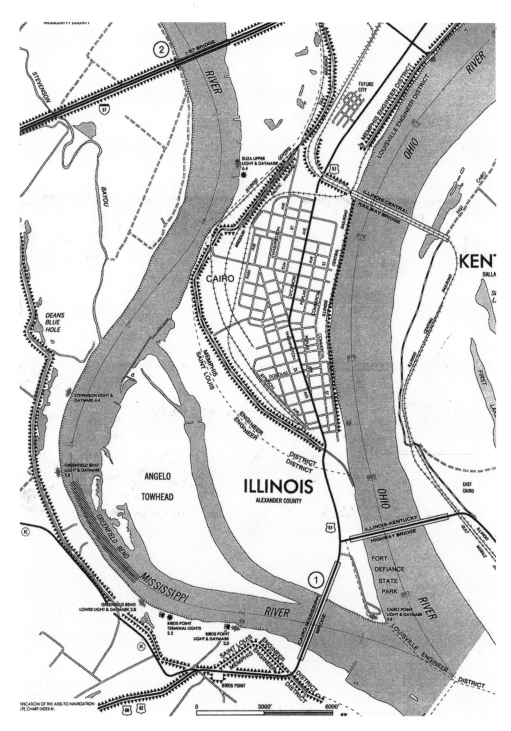

The joining of the Mississippi and Ohio Rivers

# The
# Big
# River

Confluence of the Mississippi and Ohio Rivers at the extreme southern tip of Illinois.

Everything about the lower Mississippi River was intimidating. The width of the river, the volume and power of the water, and the size of the barges.

By the time the Mississippi met the Ohio River, I had become resigned to one fact of river travel: You are never totally relaxed on the water. Day or night, one exists at a level of heightened awareness. Even after paddling 50 or 60 miles in one day and nighttime finds you exhausted, you never let yourself fall into a deep, world-be-gone sleep.

The body must find the rest it needs but the senses never seem to shut down. Throughout the night, you are aware of the changing of the winds, the barges moving up and down the river, the animals crawling around in the bushes outside the tent. You sleep. But you don't.

At the convergence of the Mississippi and Ohio rivers, I knew a geographical benchmark—another leg of the journey had been completed. But every new leg seemed accompanied by a new anxiety. I put the life jacket on a half hour before I even saw the confluence of the two rivers. Having previously experienced colliding currents, I knew this would be an attention-getting experience.

There was an awesome clashing of currents where the two great rivers met—nearly 200,000 cubic feet per second of Mississippi River water colliding with nearly 300,000 cubic feet per second of Ohio River water. I tried to stay as close to the eastern shore as possible so as not to get caught up in the middle of the current dispute. However, a large sand bar along the eastern bank of the Mississippi just above the intersection of the two rivers was forcing me out to the edge of that watery battleground. With much effort, I was was able to keep a tight hold close enough to the shore to avoid the currents. I continued paddling about 30 yards out and noticed that the current, although rolling and churning, appeared to be slow-going. After paddling about a mile near shore, I decided to venture further out to take advantage of the swifter current. The whitewater action in the middle of the river had pretty much stopped.

This was my first tactical error. My perception that the lack of whitewater meant calmer water was quickly dispelled as the first big current boil lifted me two feet high and shoved me eight feet sideways. This unexpected shove terrorized me, instantly sending me in a direction I had not been intending to go. I had become used to going downstream with the current, not across it. Needless to say, the river now had my full attention.

I paddled hard to force the kayak down river and counter the sideways motion. It seemed that as soon as I would get the craft moving forward, another boil would rise and send me to one side or the other. Sometimes a boil would rise just behind me and shoot me pleasingly forward—a movement that seemed to balance the books for the boils that would rise in front of me and bring me nearly to a stop.

My first inclination was to move back, closer to shore. But having stayed upright for the last 15 minutes in the churning Jacuzzi of a river, I was beginning to feel I was in no real danger of flipping, as long as I stayed focused. The landmarks on shore seemed to be passing at a rate that seemed faster than when I was paddling only 30 yards or so from shore. I decided to stick it out in the swifter current as long as I was confident the balance between speed and safety was at an anxiety level I could handle.

The Mississippi River was now nearly two miles wide. Above the confluence of the Ohio and Mississippi, one realized the power of the river, particularly after the Missouri joined the Mississippi above St. Louis. But nothing had prepared me for the power now on display. It was haunting at first, and it scared me. It was as if the river had tricked me into coming this far and now was testing to see just what I was really made of. Just one screw up from here on out, and I would be at the river's mercy.

I struggled for hours, keeping the kayak traveling as straight as possible. I was continually digging in hard on one side and then the other to stop or minimize a sideways push from one boil to another. It wasn't until I began to tire that I realized that the real progress was being made by the current—not by my paddling. I'm headed for the Gulf, and so is the river. Why not just go along for the ride?

It took some time before I could control my instinct to compensate for the changes in direction. However, by the end of the day I was back to the rhythmic paddling I had become so familiar with over the last 1,500 miles. The sideways pushes still caught my attention, but I had pretty much adopted a "go with the flow" attitude. Unlike smaller river paddling where a directional change may cause you to hit a rock or direct you toward a boulder or log down stream, there was nothing here to hit except the next boil.

My anxiety level was lowered by the end of the day and I was more comfortable with the company of the powerful river current. I was beginning to become more comfortable—even accustomed to the bullish current of the river. I knew, without a doubt, however, that the margin for error from here to the Gulf was far less than for any other stretch of the river I had passed through thus far.

I studied a barge coming up the river. It was large and it was loaded. The six-foot waves trailing the large craft for nearly a quarter mile were my biggest concern. They concerned me enough to put my life jacket on.

The river channel was closer than usual to the wing dam up ahead that I needed to get by. Wing dams are generally constructed of large rocks and are designed by corp of engineers to stick out into the river, somewhat perpendicular to the shore. They are meant to force water and current out into the channel.

By now I was familiar with the strong currents around such structures, and the oftentimes large whirlpools that formed on their leeward side. Some of the whirlpools had funnel holes three to four feet in diameter. They were not large enough to suck in a 17-foot kayak, but big enough to pull someone down who had been separated from his craft.

I was confident I could deal with the barge waves or the wing dam current individually. I had about a thousand miles behind me of dealing with them separately and on smaller scales. This was the first time I was going to have to deal with big current and big waves at a wing dam spill.

I gaged the distance to the wing dam, thinking I could stall until the barge waves subsided. The idea was short-lived. The current was carrying me fast; the waves were extending far behind the barge, and those waves would keep coming for some time. It seemed that my best bet was to try to pass the wing dam before the waves reached it.

For some reason on this journey, paddling back up stream and covering waters already paddled, or purposely causing an unscheduled delay was not a viable option. I instinctively adjusted and tightened the life jacket, leaned forward taking long, strong strokes, and causing the double blade paddle to bow as much as I had dared. I had to increase my speed if I was going to make it around the end of the wing dam before the waves hit the current.

It was going to be close. I was now talking to myself: 'C'mon Ron, C'mon Ron, C'mon; each repeat was said with increasing urgency. It was going to be close.

Too close! Thirty yards ahead I could see the turbulence begin. The river became like huge ski mogles instantly shifting with no pattern; class 4 whitewater with no chute. I took a rapid and hard deep breath and asked myself out loud: "What the hell, Ron, do you think you are going to live forever?"

It was a self-motivating phrase I used in tight situations to muster courage and intensify my focus. The best course of action seemed to be to paddle wide of the dam. I paddled hard on the right, deciding to swing out into the river as far as possible. The water was rougher and I was more likely to flip, but I wanted no part of the whirlpools near the wing dam if I got dumped.

I was paddling hard, trying to create distance when the kayak was instantly caught up in the crashing water. The first big wave lifted the bow skyward while another wave slammed in from the side, nearly rolling me right at the start. I caught my balance and survived several more episodes. I was about to congratulate myself when the front of the kayak dropped straight down, burying its bow in the base of a huge breaking wave. The bow disappeared as the wave crashed over the deck, slamming into me like a linebacker. Its force had nearly laid me out flat against the back deck, half taking my breath away.

I somehow managed to stay upright, maintaining balance. The kayak shed the wave. I was at maximum adrenaline and searching and waiting for what was to come next. The rodeo seem to go on for several minutes until I was carried down river below the wing dam and far enough to be away from where the strongest current was hitting the big rollers. The worst of the turbulence was over, but I was pumped.

"YES! YES! Is that all you've got?" I yelled at the river. Every sense was peaked and every muscle taut.

As quickly as the river had erupted into a frenzied battling of waves, it subsided into the calm, rolling current I had become accustomed to. My emotions took longer to settle down.

I had taken myself to the edge, a place some minutes earlier that I would have given most anything to find a way around. I had passed some test, but it had not been a battle. I learned a thousand miles back that a person cannot beat the river. The river shows no concern.

Perhaps it is as Edmund Hilary said after climbing Mount Everest: "It is not the mountain we conquer, but ourselves." In this case, it was the river. I was at a different level within myself. I had stepped up to some unknown place inside me that I had never been before. And I had left a place I can never go back to.

There have been many of those places in this journey. I needed to feel the exhilaration; to celebrate; to keep this "high" as long as I could. The routine would return soon enough.

# Marcia Sue

"A top priority of mine had been to keep as much distance as possible between the big tow boats and myself."

Since my initial encounter with a loaded barge on a narrow stretch of river near Minneapolis, Minnesota, a top priority of mine had been to keep as much distance as possible between the big tow boats and myself. For that reason, the tow boat coming up river and heading directly toward me, had my immediate attention. As I changed my course 90 degrees, I noticed a man appear on the upper deck and begin to wave. I assumed he was just acknowledging my presence and his awareness of my position out in the middle of the river.

The river was nearly a mile wide on this stretch below Baton Rouge, Louisiana and there was plenty of room to take advantage of the swifter current in the middle of the river, and still avoid the barge traffic. I waved back, like I had done to all tow boats that passed. Still, the tow kept coming directly toward me. Glancing at the name of the tow, "Marcia Sue," I got to thinking that maybe it was one of the tows I had waved to several different times up river and that this one was just swinging by for a more personal greeting.

Marcia Sue didn't register, however, and I was back to guessing what was going on. I quit paddling, trying to figure out which way to go next since I seem to be directly in its path. There were no other boats nearby so I pointed to myself, as if to question his intentions. He continued to motion for me to come toward the tow. Apparently he wanted to talk to me about something. There were a hundred potential reasons racing through my head, but none that gave reason for getting closer to that tow. Moving closer was against every procedure I had subscribed to when it came to these big boats with their engines running. I had been tossed around too many times on this journey. If this fellow thought I was going to belly up my 55 pound kayak to his big ship, he was mistaken!

As much as I enjoyed talking to people on the river, I

wanted no part of a conversation requiring me to be within talking distance of a running tow boat. I continued to drift as the tow came closer, ready to sprint out of the way if need be. It was clear—if I was not going to paddle to it, it was coming to me. At about 40 yards, I was ready to start that sprint when the captain swung the tow's stern down stream and cut the engines to low power. The tow came to dead stop in the middle of the river; he maintained just enough power to keep it from moving up river or drifting back down.

The man was now motioning more enthusiastically than ever for me to come closer. It took a critical survey of the situation before I could feel any comfort: the tow wasn't' moving, the current wasn't as bad as in some places on the river, and the guy looked friendly and obviously wanted to talk to me. As it had happened several other times on this journey, I thought, 'Heck, Ron. You think you are going to live forever?' Fifteen yards from the tow, the guy on the deck shouted above the engine's noise, "Where ya from?" I shouted "Minnesota" as I edged closer. By now the man had donned a big smile, telling me he just had to meet me.

I smiled back, but in my mind I was questioning why he was so insistent on talking with me. Then he began telling me how he had heard on the marine radio several days ago that some crazy fool was paddling down the river in a green plastic canoe. He indicated that he recalled thinking at the time how that would be about the greatest adventure he could dream of doing. When he saw me on the river today, he just had to meet me.

"They call me 'Buck,'" he said leaning over the side of the tow and sticking his hand way out for a shake. I side-paddled the remaining two yards to shake his hand and found myself in a place I thought I would never let myself be.

Another man who had climbed down the pilot's helm joined the conversation. He introduced himself as 'Stan, the captain of the tow.' By now I'm hanging onto the used truck tires that act as bumpers on the side of the tow, wondering who is minding the ship as I rapid-fire back answers to the questions they are shooting at me. After a few minutes, Stan climbed the stairs back up to the pilot's helm, making me a little less nervous knowing someone was now in charge.

Buck continued to be fascinated with the story of the journey and stated several times how much he envied me. This was a real ego builder. Here's this guy Buck, who was probably in his mid-thirties, a Marlboro man with modeling potential—a real man's man. He had a weathered river tan, bright and broad engaging smile, and was the kind of person whom I perceived to have a great, adventuresome job. And now he's telling me how much he envies me! This was worth the stop.

We were still talking when Captain Stan tooted the tow's horn, indicating the need to get back to work. Ignoring the sound, Buck asked if there were anything he could get me. I quickly responded that a cold Coke or 7-Up would be nice. Motioning to Stan to hold up for a moment, Buck disappeared into the cabin then soon returned with that big smile, a large plastic Hardees glass, a two-liter bottle of cola, and a plastic ice cream bucket full of ice. I was expecting him to pour me a glass of cola when he handed the whole works to me, asking if that was good enough.

My expression must have shown my delight. He watched as I strategically placed the glass between my lower chest and the elastic top of the spray skirt which held it in place, and the bucket of ice on the floor between my legs so it would be out of the sun. He then handed me the two-liter bottle of cola which I immediately opened and poured into the glass half way. Leaning forward so as not to spill, I placed the bottle under the cargo strap on the deck in front of me.

Buck nodded approvingly at the efficiency of the procedure and, flashing me that big smile, said I had made his day. "Same here"—I couldn't have agreed more totally.

We exchanged goodbyes as I carefully pushed off from the tow. Stan waited until I had cleared the craft by about 25 yards and then gently increased the tow's throttle, sending back a prop wash that was hardly noticeable in the Mississippi current. The Marcia Sue began moving upriver as I drifted down. Buck was still watching me from the deck and waved one last time before disappearing into the cabin. I took a few paddles to maneuver the kayak into a parallel line with the current to smooth the ride and prepared myself for a little refreshment.

I glanced back up river, partly for safety reasons and partially to take a last glimpse of the Marcia Sue. The tow was well up river now, and already "history" for this trip. Like so many other times on this journey, the words from the song, "Proud Mary," rolled through my mind, triggering my short, but loud and off-key rendition of Credence Clearwater Revival singing the song. As always, I emphasized the lines, "People on the river are happy to give."

Between paddling and singing I finished the first glass of cola as the last of the ice in the glass melted. Either the time flew by or the ice melted awfully fast. Most likely, it was the latter, since it is a well-known fact in Louisiana that ice doesn't last long outdoors in July. While preparing another glass, I wrapped my rain suit around the ice bucket to give it some added insulation. I knew I was going to have to drink that pop quickly if I was going to enjoy it cold.

The pop felt cool and refreshing against my chest where the elastic top of the spray skirt held it firmly while I paddled. I was already rehashing the encounter with Buck, Stan, and the Marcia Sue, thinking as I paddled, 'good people, good pop, good weather.' This was going to be a good day.

# Pilot
# Town

Main Street

LOUISIANA

MISSISSIPPI

NEW ORLEANS ○

VENICE ○
PILOTTOWN
HEAD OF PASSES
RIVER MILE MARKER ZERO

GULF OF MEXICO

It was two days before the end. I was paddling "thin." Thin meant I was low on supplies. The 25 pounds of food I had started with—and occasionally replenished through the generosity of the people on the river was almost gone—two suppers and three breakfasts remained, but the only lunch items left on my table consisted of a few granola bars and couple onion buns I had scored from some fishermen two days earlier.

Ahead of me, fishing from a rock revetment on a levy, were a young black woman and two children. I decided to paddle over to them and ask if there might be a convenience store or market close by on the back side of the levy where I might buy some lunch supplies.

All three watched as I paddled down river. I suspected that a person in a kayak was a rare sight on this part of the river and that perhaps they might be very interested in the kayak and the story. I was even thinking they might be interested enough to watch my craft while I shopped or, preferably, perhaps one might volunteer to go purchase the lunches I needed.

All of my "hope-fors" and "maybes" became "no-ways" when the kayak turned in their direction. They lifted their cane poles out of the water, grabbed the bucket sitting between them, scrambled up the revetment, and disappeared over the top without stopping to look back. A quick shout of "Wait, don't go," had zero effect on their retreat. Staring at the now-vacant bank, I drifted for awhile thinking, 'Now that was different.' I wondered what experiences they must have had that caused them to react like that.

This was a first for me; to have my appearance so obviously frighten or cause someone to retreat was unsettling. During the journey I had begun to envision myself as a smiling, non-threatening traveler who was willing to stop and share 'the story.' I wondered why this had happened; and why, since it hadn't happened before, that it was happening now. (I had established early on, and have long since become accustomed to the fact that a solo journey down the river allows way too much time to think!)

I was now 120 miles from Head of the Passes. This is the name of the location of the Mississippi River Mile Marker Zero. It marks the official beginning of the Mississippi River navigational system and the end of the 2,552 mile journey for me. It was still two full, but hopefully easy days of paddling from where I was right now. Two more nights of sleeping on the ground—maybe three at the most.

It was mid-afternoon and I had spent the better part of the day dodging barge traffic. It was obvious that the closer I got to New Orleans, the busier the river shipping traffic was becoming. By now, I was somewhat comfortable with being able to stay out of the way of the big tow boats and ships. The difference now, was that there were a lot of them. Keeping track of all the moving barges' directions and speeds required most of my concentration. Tow boats were moving barges up river, down river—and back and forth across the river. Paddling outside the channel markers, I was less concerned with the barges going up and down than I was with the tows moving them back and forth.

The riverbank from Baton Rouge to New Orleans appeared to be one long anchorage warehouse for barges waiting to be loaded or unloaded at some point on the river. It was amazing how any barge company could identify or keep track of where their barges were kept. The huge, rusty hulks of floating warehouses all looked the same to me.

It was late afternoon by the time I reached river mile marker 115 near Ama, Louisiana. Believing the shipping traffic would only get worse the closer I got to New Orleans, I had decided to find a safe campsite as close to the city as possible, get up early, and then try to paddle through New Orleans before the shipping workday began. It was probably a three to four-hour paddle to go the 20-mile distance needed to get through that busy port city. I was hoping that an early camp and good night's rest would give me the spirit and strength for a sprint through New Orleans.

By early evening, I had located a good, high, dry campsite on the north bank of the river, several hundred yards down river from the Huey P. Long Bridge. The campsite was below the levy crest and for the most part, out of direct sight from just about everywhere but the river. It felt pretty comfortable.

The barge traffic continued during the night and awakened me several times. I wondered if it were going to let up at all by morning. I woke just prior to daybreak and, watching the river while I made breakfast, it was evident the river traffic was considerably less than yesterday afternoon. Perhaps my strategy was going to work. By 8:30 I had cleared the main part of the city port and reached the U.S. Naval activity area on the down river side of the city. I was past the city port area and headed for Venice, Louisiana. Venice is nearly a 90 mile drive down river from New Orleans. It is the last town out on the delta that a person can drive to. It is also the location where I was to meet my wife Lila for the return ride home. That last 90 miles down river was still a day and a half-paddle. I had plenty of time to pray that Lila would be there.

The early and fast start effort to get through New Orleans found me 62 miles down river from last night's camp and only 43 miles from the end. It was 5:30 P.M. and, knowing I should have an easy days paddle to reach Venice tomorrow, I began looking for a good campsite for my last night on the river. The thought gave me mixed emotions.

I found a level camping spot on a piece of shoreline about two feet above river level. It was flat, dry, and open to the breeze. About as good a spot as I could hope for on this last night of the journey. Reaching into the food bag I grabbed the last remaining pasta dinner and stared into the now, almost empty bag. Three instant oatmeal packets and the last foil-wrapped onion roll were the bags only contents. The finality of my journey was registering with each "last." The last 42 miles, the last campsite, the last dinner, and now I was staring at the last breakfast.

The coffee supply was probably the only part of this journey that would not see an end. There was plenty left. The weather had been so hot on the lower end of the river that hot coffee hadn't been part of many meals. Although the calm, humid, 80-degree evening air was far from chilling, I wrapped both hands around a warm mug of it. It was somehow a soothing and comforting feeling. I sat on the bank like I had so many evenings, staring out at the river, mesmerized by the rolling and swirling current as it tried to conclude its journey to the Gulf.

Tonight was different. The coffee smelled richer, the river was calmer, and my thoughts were deeper than at any other time. Most evenings hadn't left time or energy for major contemplation. The ritual was eat, bathe, stow the gear and sleep—with maybe just a bit of think-time about the next day.

Tonight I found myself passing through the past days' events and giving thought to the miles, the people, the encounters—to the guy who started the journey and the one who was finishing it.

The hour-long riverbank meditation had an energizing effect. Lying on the sleeping bag in my tent, I was far from sleepy. Maybe it was the anticipation of tomorrow, seeing my wife again, and having a soft bed and a cooked meal. But I knew it was something more. Not so much a feeling "about" something as it was "of" something. I wondered how much richer the trip might have been had I not, each evening, put so much emphasis on making another five miles before day's end.

I woke early on this last morning and made breakfast with the last three packets of oatmeal. The extra packet was my insurance of extra energy needed to get me the last 42 miles to Venice. There was only the lonely onion roll on the menu for lunch.

The morning was clear and calm, the current good, the wind good, and the kayak responded well. I was happy with the world this morning and the day was going to go quickly. By 3:30 I was paddling into Venice. I was surprised at how much commercial fishing boat and recreational boat traffic there was for such a small town. I later learned that the town's major commerce was seafood and supply support for the offshore oil industry.

I paddled into Grand Pass, an off-shoot of the river channel that provides easy access to the Gulf for the commercial fishing boats and that leads to the town's wharf area. A Vietnamese fishing crew were interested in my passing and peered over the side of their boat as I paddled by. I asked where I might find a public phone and they pointed out the Coast Guard Office, as well as asked their own questions about the kayak and my trip. The station was easily visible as I pulled the kayak up onto the freshly mowed lawn of the station ground. A tingle of exhilaration shot through me. Another benchmark had been reached. I was at the last town on the river that could be reached by automobile; it was the place I would return to once I had reached the end of the river. In a sense, Venice would be the end of the journey, after the end of the journey.

I made a call to my father's home in Illinois. He was to be the information coordinator between my wife and I. Lila was to have left Minnesota four days earlier to pick up her sister in Illinois who was to be her traveling companion on her way to pick me up in Venice. Several days back I had asked Buck, the crewman on the tow Marcia Sue, to call my father and let him know I would be in Venice in three days and that I would call him when I reached the town. Lila was then to call my father to find out the latest of my where-abouts.

Buck apparently was a man of his word. When my father picked up the phone he said, "I knew it would be you!" He said he'd had a short chat with Buck three days ago. Lila had gotten the word and the plans were that she would reach Venice this evening. I told dad my pickup point would be the U.S. Coast Guard Station.

After two ready-made sandwiches, a candy bar, and three Cokes from the vending machines in the station waiting area, I rounded up the kayak and gear and moved it to the front of the station grounds where I could watch the entrance. When evening set in, I made a call to my go-between father again and got the update that Lila would be in Venice in two hours. Oh, the joy!

The next morning was tough. The mental turmoil of how to end the trip had been brewing the evening before. For the first time in many mornings, a convenient and viable option for not paddling existed. The kayak was strapped to the roof of the car, the gear was stowed in the trunk, and I was showered and wearing fresh, clean clothes. Perhaps this was the time to call it the end.

I had paddled 2,542 miles; what difference would 10 more

miles make. If I paddled the last 10 miles down to Mile Marker "0" I would then have to paddle back up river the same 10 miles to get back to Venice and the car. Ten miles down and 10 back against the current would be like another 30 miles and take most of a day. Or, perhaps I could just paddle out one of the several short two to three mile cutoff passes to the Gulf and call it a trip—Headwaters to the Gulf.

The breakfast discussion continued along this vein. I wanted to go home. Badly. I was tired of paddling. The end wasn't supposed to be like this. It was supposed to be a celebration; but I wasn't celebrating. I couldn't end the journey like this. There had to be a better feeling. I told Lila I needed to go back to the river; to finish my original journey and not some modified version. I had to finish what I had started.

Before getting into the kayak, I told Lila and her sister Sue I would try to be back by midafternoon. I was paddling thin, with only water, lunch, and a life jacket. The rest of the gear remained packed in the car. It felt odd, like I was under-equipped to be on the river, unprepared to survive the river. I turned and waved as they stood and watched me head to that magnetic Mile Marker Zero that had drawn the kayak to it from 2,552 miles away.

I was refreshed and paddling the light kayak with ease down the river, but it seemed prudent to conserve energy, not yet knowing what it would take to get back up river. Within an hour I approached a place on the east shore that the map identified as Pilot Town. Ahead, sitting at the end of a pier was and fisherman. I asked him if he knew which of the landforms that could be seen two miles down river might be closest to navigational Mile Marker Zero. I didn't want to do any more paddling than I had to. He pointed out two land forms and channel markers that would guide me, adding that he was a river pilot

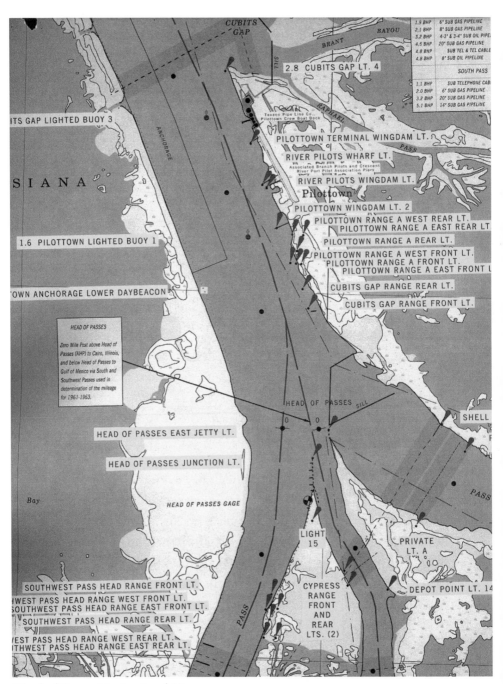

Head of Passes Navigational Map

who stayed at Pilot Town while he was working. As I began to paddle away, he invited me to stop on the way back for a cold pop at the pilot's house. He said to just ask anyone where the house was and they would point it out.

Two miles down river from Pilot Town, the mighty Mississippi River ends at Head of the Passes. Here the river splits into three separate smaller channels. They are Pass A Lourte, South Pass, and Southwest Pass. Only South Pass and Southwest Pass are used by ocean going ship traffic. Southwest Pass is maintained to a depth of 45 feet and continues for another 18 miles below Mile Marker Zero, out into the Gulf.

Head of The Passes channel marker locates navigational mile marker zero on the Mississippi River and the end of the my 2,552 mile journey.

Within 20 minutes of leaving Pilot Town I was pulling the kayak up onto the 2-foot high rock jetty stretching up river from the land form that separated Pass A Lourte from South Pass and directly east of Mile Post Zero. The lighted navigational tower at the end of the jetty was identified as the Head Of the Passes East jetty Light. It was the closest thing I would find to an end of the journey monument so I took a picture of it.

Sitting down on the rocks next to the kayak, I began like I had started so many other days—talking to the kayak.

'What do you think? Not exactly the joyous, champagne, fireworks ending I had imagined it might be.'

Somehow, talking to the little craft, even though it was a chunk of plastic, made me feel like I was talking with a team member, a partner—not just to myself. We had journeyed 2,552 miles and both been tested to our structural limits. Independently, we had each held up our end of the deal to complete the journey. Admittedly, I ended each of these conversations with a reality check: 'Ron, do you realize you are talking to a piece of plastic?'

I am not sure how long I sat, staring in the direction of the river that I had been journeying for nearly 44 days. But all the scenes and encounters that began at the Headwaters of Lake Itasca, to the immediate vision of the huge bow of an ocean-going ship that just appeared to my left, took their turn going through my mind again. Edmond Hillary wrote, after his successful climb of Mt. Everest: "It is not the mountain we conquer, but ourselves." Perhaps for the first time I not only understood, but could feel what he meant.

The ship coming from behind me from the Southwest Pass signaled again the ever-present alertness to potential danger on the river. It also brought me back to the fact that the journey was not over yet and I need to stay alert. Knowing the big ship

would be making large waves, I figured that the two-foot high rock jetty might not be the driest place to be when they hit.

I was far out into the river when the kayak began to rise and fall with each crest and trough of the big waves created by the passing ship. I grinned, knowing that may have been my last encounter with one of the big ships. It took me nearly 40 minutes to paddle the two miles back up river to Pilot town. That meant it would take about three hours to go the remaining eight miles to Venice. Stopping at Pilot Town for the promised cold soda would delay me about a half hour, but give me a chance to see this unique community.

Pilot Town can be accessed only by boat or helicopter. I chose what looked like one of the main constructed channels into the town area. One side was lined with docks and fishing boats and terminated at a grassy end by an elevated concreted walkway. I asked a young fishermen where I would find the River Pilots House and he pointed down a walkway, indicating it was the third house on the street.

One of the main boat canals leading into Pilot Town. Pilot Town can only be reached by boat or helicopter.

I pulled the kayak up on the dry dirt bank and climbed up on the four-foot high elevated walkway and looked around. Not seeing any roads I shouted back to the boy "How far to the street?" He answered: "You are standing on it. That's the street!"

The walkway, I mean the street, was five feet wide with a railing always on one side and sometimes on both. It was elevated about four feet above the ground as far as I could see in either direction. All the houses were elevated about four or six feet above ground and connected to the street by elevated sidewalks. Most of the houses were large, two or three story buildings painted white with big palm trees, pine trees, satellite dishes and/or radio towers in the front yards, four feet below the elevated streets and sidewalks.

I headed for the third house and walked up on the spacious, full length porch and knocked on the door. A fellow who was not Jim answered. When I asked for Jim and told him I had been promised a cold drink, I was told Jim wasn't in but I was more than welcome to the soda. He introduced himself as Mark and showed me the large restaurant style kitchen where he took my soda from a large, stainless steel refrigerator. He showed me where all the fixings were for making lunch and told me to help myself while he did some business on the radio. The full breakfast at the cafe in Venice this morning was wearing thin so I made a generous sandwich.

Access to all buildings in Pilot Town was elevated walkways. Some yards were fenced to keep out unwanted critters. The difference between high ground and river level seemed to be no more than 2-3 feet over most of the town area.

When Mark returned, he showed me the remainder of the large house, pointing out how high up on the second story the storm surge water level had risen during hurricane Camille. He said the house was the place where several river pilots stayed at a time while they were doing their duty term. The ocean-going ships would anchor in designated areas where they would be boarded by a river pilot. Ocean going ship pilots were not permitted to operate their ships in the Mississippi River system. It had something to do with territorial protocol between ocean pilots and river pilots, and the skills needed to navigate in strong river currents.

Once the ocean going ships reached Pilot Town, a river pilot who was on duty staying at the house was assigned to the ship and guided it up river to its port, and back down river to Pilot town where the river pilot would then return the ship to the ocean pilot and exit the ship. The river pilot would return to the house and wait for the next ship assignment.

We chatted for awhile and then Mark asked if I needed a ride back. I didn't take him seriously and added that I had a 17-foot kayak to take back to Venice with me. Mark said that taking the craft back on the boat would not be a problem; that it would easily fit on the forward deck of the transport boat. I finally realized he wasn't talking about one of the recreational cabin cruisers or fishing boats I had seen docked along the channel. He was describing the large transport boat that runs daily between Venice and Pilot Town, carrying day visitors, pilot family members, and supplies.

I was willing! Mark said he would let the boat pilot know I would be returning with the boat and told me to have my gear at the end of the pier by 2:30 P.M.

I carried the kayak down the elevated street and to the end of the pier. There was a large grey boat, about 50 feet long, tied to the end of the pier. It was my ride back to Venice. I stood looking down river at the Head Of the Passes, especially aware of the dangers that had been spared me. Operating at heightened awareness had been a constant on this journey. With the concern for safety slowly draining away, I was experiencing a hollow feeling; an empty emotional space; an unsettling feeling. Up until now, each day had a single purpose, single focus, and that was to reach Navigational Mile Marker Zero safely. It had been done and the journey's end was now a 15 minute boat ride away.

The kayak fit easily on the bow, leaving ample room for the seven other passengers. Some asked questions about the journey on the way to Venice and I enthusiastically answered as many as I could during the trip. This, perhaps, was part of the celebration.

I was again greeted with smiles and hugs from Lila and Sue. There was a joy in my wife's eyes that said so much. This was the celebration!

Testing the straps that held the kayak to the car I turned and took one last look at the river. Smiling, I thought, 'You did it. You went to the end. No abbreviations. No stops short of Mile Marker Zero.

Each crossing of the Mississippi River on the trip back caused a story to be told about the day I passed that spot, or that campsite, or the people I met along the way. Perhaps this too, was part of the celebration. If so, it never ends.

When I look at that picture, I am there. I feel myself back on the river and a calmness settles in.

# Afterword

It is 8 P.M. as I begin writing, and all is well in the world outside my office window near Cloquet, Minnesota—some 75 miles from the nearest bank of the Mississippi River.

On the wall next to my desk hangs a picture of a sunset on the river. In a cloudless sky, the pale yellow, marble-sized sun sets against a pastel horizon. It silhouettes a tree line some far distance down the river. The sun's silver-grey reflection off the river water contrasts decisively with the dull, dark colors of the sandbar shoreline on which I have camped.

When I look at that picture on the wall, I can smell the many scents of river water—the musty aroma of moist soil and decaying vegetation along the bank. And I can hear the ominous creaking sound and feel the thundering vibration of chamber doors closing behind me at the locks that I traveled through. I can see the barges coming around the bend in the river up ahead. I can hear the low rumble of engines as they churn their way up river in the middle of the night.

I hear doves cooing just beyond the levee; cooing in cadence with the nearly silent rhythmic dipping of the paddle in the calmness of early morning.

When I look at that picture, I am there. I feel myself back on the river and a calmness settles in. If my supervisors knew how often 'I am there,' they would make me take that picture down!

I often catch myself reflecting on the words of Sir Arthur Conan Doyle, a famous early 20th century Scottish author/ adventurer who said: "There's many a man who never tells his adventures, for he can't hope to be believed. Who's to blame them? For this will seem a bit of a dream to ourselves in a month or two."

I am amazed at how quickly one is absorbed into the work-day world, where once again we walk the treadmill of productivity, striving to meet the demands of society. I am equally amazed at how quickly the days pass, and how rapidly events of the past are distanced from the present. Perhaps life passed equally as fast at the turn of the century. I am fortunate, however, for I have the brakes to the treadmill—it is hanging on the wall next to my desk. Each time I pick up the picture and step into it, the treadmill stops. . . until I return from the river.

There are two kinds of people who ask questions about the journey: The "Wows" are the first group. These folks are the ones whose eyes widen and whose faces brighten with smiles. I can sense the questions building in their minds, and then those questions come in rapid fire. If there are several "Wows" in the group, trying to answer is like trying to get a drink out of a fire hose. Their excitement is infectious. After the initial barrage of questions, my answers become more detailed—a performance of sorts, and with each new question, another act.

The Wows wish they had been with me on the journey, or wish they could someday do it themselves. Most of the people I met on the river were Wows.

The other category is the "Whys." Whenever I encounter a Why, a puzzled look comes across their faces, followed by a question: 'Why would you ever want to do something like that?'

The first couple times I met a Why, I was caught off guard. I wasn't sure how to answer. I had never asked myself the question. When asked, I answered the Why simply by saying it just seemed like a fun and exciting thing to do; something I had dreamed about doing for many years.

I suspect that everyone has a list of things they would like to accomplish during their lifetimes, things that will make their lives fuller or richer in some way. To borrow a line from Henry David Thoreau's "Walden" in which he speaks of why he went to the woods, "Because I wished to live deliberately. And not, when I came to die, discover that I had not lived." Paddling the Mississippi River had always been high on my list. Try as I might, however, it seems I could never convince the "Whys" of the world that it was a great adventure.

After many conversations about the journey, it was fascinating to study the response of people when the subject of the journey came up. It was immediately apparent by the look on their faces who the "Wows" were and who the "Whys" were. The Wows never could get enough information—and they never asked 'why.' The Whys, on the other hand, seemed never to understand—no matter how I tried to explain it. Perhaps the commonality between the two groups was that they were just plain interested in what I got out of it, albeit for far different reasons.

What DID I get out of the adventure? I don't think anyone could experience the unsolicited kindness that I received from people along the way, without returning as a kinder and more giving person.

I don't think a person can endure the physical hardship of 2,552 miles of river paddling and not return as a more self-confident person. A solo traveler could not survive the day after day, endless hours of uninterrupted thinking and not return with a more open mind. One cannot witness the natural beauty of the river and feel its timelessness, and not return with a greater sense of wonder. Being on a journey changes a person. It is inevitable.

The most frequently asked question is: 'What was the biggest change in yourself?' My answer varies with my mood. My first thought is to admit that the thing I was least prepared to handle was the amount of time spent thinking. Just thinking. No one to talk to; nothing to do except paddle. So you are always thinking. Combine all that thinking with the timelessness of the river and and you end up thinking a lot about your place in the universe.

The river seems to communicate that it does not care about time; that it is eternal; that not long after our society has flourished and failed, it will erase our efforts to control it and turn to wandering where it chooses—as it has done for thousands of years.

You sense your existence is but a speck on the river's timeline. It's a humbling experience. I came away with a new perspective on life, and a different perception of what is important in that life. Without a doubt, I am back on society's treadmill. But now I regularly step off to revisit the river via that picture on the wall—to see, smell, and feel the water; to refuel the calmness and not lose perspective.

People usually ask, 'what's next on the list?' It's a tough question because the list is not carved in stone. It is more of an opportunistic list where, if an opportunity to enjoy life presents itself, the opportunity is taken. The list is not a scorecard where adventures get crossed off as they are completed. And it's not an awards list, where you win only if you complete the list before you are too old or you die.

The list exists only as a reminder to enjoy life first, and not when it comes time to die—discover that you have not lived.